THE RAVEN

EPISODE

IV-VI

TOBEY ALEXANDER

ADVENTURE CALLS
**TAGS
CREATIVE**
PUBLISHING TEAM

TAGS CREATIVE

— • —

EPISODE

IV

FULL MOON

1

TRADITIONS

'How can you see this as a success?' Diana boomed into the phone as she paced her office. 'I don't care what you have to do. Find him!'

Ending the call, Diana dropped the phone into her pocket and slumped into her seat. Closing her eyes, she took a deep breath before turning her attention to the figure sat in the room's corner. Dressed in an immaculately tailored suit, as always, Qamar offered her a knowing grin as he sipped from his cup of tea.

'I'd never have thought a Revenant would speak on the phone.'

'Get a grip!' Diana snapped. 'That's the team that is with them.'

'I guessed that. I also assume there's no progress in finding him?'

'Nothing, even the Revenants are drawing a blank. It's like he's simply disappeared.'

'You don't think that they have given him passage beyond believing he has honoured his oath, do you?'

'While they cannot interfere, there's no way they don't know the truth about The Ripper.'

'Then he must be somewhere.' Qamar finished his drink and placed the ornate cup on the table in front of him. 'Perhaps we could explore alternative methods to draw him out.'

'Such as?'

'We could begin the ritual early, see if the scent of the real Ripper doesn't bring him to us.'

'Is that wise?'

The question lingered in the office for a moment as Qamar span his coin on the tabletop. Spinning it and slamming his hand down on the ornate coin. Checking which way it had landed, Qamar sighed and slumped back in his seat. Clearly unhappy with the result, he slid the coin into his palm and admired the intricate detail of the demon's face, and collected his thoughts.

'You're probably right.' He offered at last. 'I would have thought you would have all the answers, having had him in this place for so long.'

'He was here by his own choice.'

'At first!' Qamar interrupted.

'Yes, and that's why he locked himself away. When he sensed the changes and the idea of freedom slipping from his grasp, John closed himself down to all of us.'

'Except the girl,' Qamar offered with a raised eyebrow. 'She did exactly what you wanted her to do, awaken the embers to take flame again.'

'She hasn't seen him.' Diana groaned as she turned to look out of the office window 'We would know if he had made contact.'

'Could we not use her as the beacon to bring him back?'

'I've toyed with the idea, but I'm not sure he's as tied to her as we believe. He isn't aware of the full truth yet.'

'Maybe we should make him aware.'

'John isn't the type of creature to be fooled easily.'

'He would be more of a fool not to believe it.'

Mulling over the idea, Diana took a moment to decide how they should proceed. Ever since maneuvering herself into a prominent position within the Full Moon Society, Qamar had often vetoed her ideas in open forum. Very much a stamp of his authority. His sudden consideration and reliance on her was a feeling she wished to savour for however long it would last. Despite having been John's keeper at the Nuthall Hospital for so long, she knew nothing about his nature. Well, that wasn't entirely true, she knew his origins but not the depth and breadth of his powers. John had always played that part of himself down, despite her attempts to tease elements out of him over the years.

'We could let the truth about Kimberley be revealed, I'm sure he has ears in the right places. I would expect that alone would bring him to her.'

'Is there something about this woman that you worry about putting her in danger?' Qamar teased as he moved across the office towards Diana. 'You seem reluctant to put her in danger. Any reason for that?'

'Only that violence isn't always necessary.' Qamar raised an eyebrow at her snapped reply. 'Besides, John would be more likely to walk away if he saw such a sudden change in behaviour towards her.'

'While you're right, I don't think it's the reason for your reluctance.' Qamar tapped his coin on the desk three times. 'But I'm willing to play along.'

Making his declaration, Qamar tossed the coin in the air and caught it before turning and stalking towards the door. Remaining in her seat, Diana watched as he pulled the door open and stalked out into the corridor, slamming the door behind him. Letting out a long sigh, Diana leaned back in her chair and stared up at the ceiling.

'Arrogant bastard!' She groaned. 'I haven't come this far to be brushed aside by people like him.'

Pulling her phone from her pocket, Diana unlocked it and searched through the contacts. Finding Kimberley's name, she tapped the dial icon and placed the phone down on her desk. Activating the hands free, it filled the room with the sound of the call as it connected and started ringing. After a handful of rings, the phone was diverted to voicemail. When the pre-recorded message had finished, Diana recorded a short voicemail.

'Call me back however you see fit. We need to talk, and while I know you don't trust me. This is my private number, it'll just be me and you.' Ending the call, Diana rose from her seat and moved to the window overlooking the Nuthall Hospital courtyard.

For what felt like an age, Diana paced the large office, hoping Kimberley would return her call. At last, the room was filled with the vibrations of the phone as it danced across the desk. Seeing the anonymous caller ID, Diana knew it would be Kimberley, and quickly answered the call.

'You've got a nerve.' Kimberley snapped over the speaker.

'Lets not play games, Kimberley. We need to talk.'

'Then talk.'

'Not over the phone, in person.'

'You want me to risk everything and meet you?' Kimberley laughed down the line. 'You've been spending too much time with your own inmates.'

'Funny choice of words, inmates.' Diana hissed as she slid back into the comfort of her seat. 'Only a few months ago you referred to them in quite a different way.'

'That's before I knew what your hospital was about.'

'Come now, John is just a single entity in this place.' Diana toyed with her own coin as she spoke. 'You saw them as little more than curiosities for your research.'

'That was until I saw the truth.'

'Truth from his perspective. Please, don't tell me you've fallen for those puppy-dog eyes and swallowed everything he's told you as gospel.'

'What do you want?' Kimberley snapped, ending the conversation.

'Like I said, we need to talk.'

''Talk then.'

'You really are a difficult woman!' Diana snapped as she span the coin on the desk. 'Consider the fact I called your mobile. If we were tracking you, then we would have found you already.'

'Where?' Kimberley sighed.

'I'll make it public, so you can feel more comfortable. Trafalgar Square?'

'Sunset.' Kimberley barked and ended the call.

Rolling her eyes, Diana couldn't help but admire the tenacity of the woman. It wasn't surprising, but what would follow next would be a delicate balancing act. She knew John, or better now The Raven, would most likely be watching Kimberley but would remain in the shadows. She knew the Revenants would be able to sniff out Death's Hand, but even a hint of treachery and he would disappear again.

Diana knew this meeting would need to be just her. Choosing such a public place had been deliberate, hoping that John would see their meeting, Diana trusted it would sew enough doubt in Kimberley's true allegiance to bring him out of the shadows. Keeping the Revenants contained and away from the meeting would add to the web she was spinning.

Pleased with herself, Diana flicked the coin into the air and allowed it to clatter to the floor by the side of her chair. Allowing it to settle, she eventually looked down and smiled as the demonic face on the coin looked up at her. Having decided her course of action, she checked the time and, once she had collected the coin, made her way out of the office and down into the hospital bowels.

Navigating her way to John's room was an instinct. Offering curt nods to the guards and staff as she moved into the older wing of the hospital, she placed her card against the reader and pushed open the solid door. Since John's dramatic escape, she had ordered the old wing emptied of residents, not wanting them to see hope in John's display of strength.

'Do you want me to leave you alone?' The gruff orderly that had accompanied Kimberley was sitting in the small security office.

'No, it's fine.' Diana dismissed the dark bruises that covered his face. 'You can make sure nobody disturbs me.'

'Not a problem.' The man replied as she walked along the corridor.

Moving towards the interview room, Diana felt a swell of admiration for the damage to the wall and door. She knew the dampening bracelets had worked to contain John's powers, but she had not expected such a surge in the moments of him being released from them. With everything still in situ, Diana stepped over the threshold and quickly found one of the dampening bracelets amongst the dust and debris from the shattered brick-work.

'All that power, contained by something so small.' Diana mused as she admired the silverware.

Looking like nothing that belonged in a prison, the bracelet almost looked to be a piece of gothic jewelery. A jet-black stone sat in the centre of the bracelet and she saw her own reflection on the polished surface. Even in the dim light of the former interview room, Diana could see the swirling smoke beneath the glassy surface of the gemstone.

Not understanding how the bracelets worked, John had surrendered them when he had voluntarily presented at the Nuthall Hospital in the early eighties. The former warden, unassociated to the Full Moon Society, the warden had been an honest man. It was until the mid-nineties that the Society had maneuvered their pieces to remove him from his office and allow Diana to be elevated into her current position.

Mystified by the bracelet's nature, Diana had never been able to hold it or even admire it as close as she was now. Under no circumstances had they been able to remove them from John without risking his powers returning, as they had done now. To hold the weighty silver item in her hand, she wondered what was contained within it, what magic bound John into nothing more than an empty shell of an undying man.

'How does this all work?' She mused as she admired the bracelet. 'Something so small.'

Not wanting to leave the second bracelet behind, Diana set about searching the rubble-strewn floor for the matching bracelet. Having watched the video of their interaction, she had seen how Kimberley had released John from his binds. Knowing it had been necessary, it still bore a frustration that she had not been able to control John enough to set the prophecy in motion. Instead, she had been forced to rely upon one not borne of the Society, Kimberley.

'A burnt jewel, a hell demons throne. Both twins will meet a fight.' Diana hushed as she dusted off the second bracelet. 'The prophecy will be fulfilled.'

Leaving the destruction behind, Diana left the quiet interview room and prepared to meet Kimberley.

2

A SENTINEL'S PERCH

The Raven sat amongst the shadows of the building with a view onto Trafalgar Square. He had surveyed the surrounding streets and sensed no sign of any Revenants or creatures of darkness. In the days since defeating The Ripper, John could not detect much in the way of darkness tracing through the capital's streets. Finding a place to sit, John rested against an enormous gargoyle and watched the sun setting behind London's skyline.

Every inch of him wanted to challenge Kimberley as she waited at the base of Nelson's Column, but he knew better than to act in haste. Having watched her from afar, John had not chanced speaking with her since leaving the hospital. He had seen her enough to know she was safe, but now he wondered if it had been the right choice to let her be so far from him. Catching only parts of the conversations, John had chanced a connection with Kimberley in the street not moments before.

As she had navigated the busy underground network, John had merged with the crowds, and while he could never shield himself from her view, the anonymity provided by the sea of faces had been enough. Knowing she was forever conscious of his existence, the dark magic that could shroud him from other people's consciousness no longer affected her. Pushing through the tightly packed platform, all he had needed was the lightest of touches as their paths crossed to steal a fleeting glimpse of her memory.

Brushing his fingertips against the back of her hand, his mind had navigated to the conversation with Diana and the anger had surged through him. Seeing her flinch, John had watched her from a distance without showing himself. Blending with the commuters and tourists, Kimberley had scanned the crowds before boarding the packed underground train. As the grime-covered carriages pulled out of the station, John felt the anger boiling inside him. Knowing he was concealed from view, he dropped from the platform and onto the lines.

Hearing the rumble of trains along the labyrinth of snaking tunnels that passed over and under one another, John made quick work of navigating the tunnel away from the platform. Finding a small access hatch, he pulled it open and made his way into the service tunnels that ran alongside the primary tunnels.

'This feels much more like home.' John had remarked as he made his way back to the long forgotten underground station.

Having stolen the memory, John watched what he could in the confines of an old, abandoned train carriage and made his choice. Hours later, he found himself hidden among the shadows, eagerly waiting for the meeting between Kimberley and Diana. The sun bathed John in its blood-red glow as it descended behind the distant horizon and skyline. Admiring the curious glow of his coat, John called the plague doctor mask to his hand and admired the intricacy of its design.

Having found the old Victorian underground station, a relic of a familiar past, John had felt he once again belonged. The world had changed so much and yet he had not. Although he had been part of the evolution of modern London, he had never felt part of it. It had been one reason he had surrendered to the Nuthall, to find a place that allowed him to feel he was not an outcast.

Admiring the leather and copper detailing of the mask, he realised he had never changed his external representation of The Raven. The mask itself had been a whim, no sense or reason other than a story his mother had told him as a child, but the coat, that was different. The long leather coat looked battered and worn, yet he would not have it any other way. It had been a gift from his wife, before he had died, and it had been the one thing he had taken with him when Death had taken John's path.

Distracted by his own reminiscing, John returned his attention to the world below and jumped to his feet as Diana sauntered down the steps from the National Gallery. His senses tingled as he watched Diana almost float down the steps and march across the paved square towards Kimberley. Seeing them together filled him with anger and despite himself, John placed the plague doctor mask over his face.

Ever cautious that both women were consciously aware of his presence, John considered moving closer to hear what was being discussed between the two of them. Knowing he would compromise himself, all he could do was watch and wait. As the two women talked, he could see Kimberley was on edge. While she kept her distance from Diana, she was scanning the surrounding crowds, as if expecting someone else to arrive.

'This'll be interesting.' John hushed to himself as the discussion grew more animated.

Whatever had been said, it riled Kimberley. As Diana thrust a handful of paperwork into her hands, Kimberley pulled away. Staring at the pages, John could almost see the look of pleasure on Diana's face as the colour drained from Kimberley's. Watching her read the paperwork, his impatience grew as he longed to know what the two colluding women were talking about.

'No!'

Even from his perch high above, Kimberley's voice carried on the wind to where he was hidden. John tensed as he watched Kimberley launch the handful of sheets back at Diana, spilling them onto the paved square. Ignored by the people who walked around them, Diana did not pick up the sheets as the gentle breeze sent most of them tumbling into the churning water of the fountains.

Their meeting was over. John watched as Kimberley turned from Diana and stalked away towards the steady flow of traffic. Following Kimberley, John eventually returned his attention to Diana and froze in place when his gaze settled back on her. Diana's attention was fixed exactly where he was standing amongst the shadows of the elaborate rooftop.

Unsure if she had seen him, John did not dare move. Feeling her gaze probing the dark shadows, he pressed back against the cold stone and waited to see if she really had seen him. Making sure his senses were tuned to the approach of any creatures connected to the afterlife, he half expected to feel the familiar presence of a Revenant somewhere nearby, but felt nothing. After what felt like an age, Diana turned away from him and stormed back across Trafalgar Square towards the impressively ornate National Gallery.

Satisfied she had gone, John made sure he was unseen by the world and dropped from the rooftop. Landing on the pavement, the world moved around John, oblivious to his presence as he expertly navigated the flow of people without breaking a stride. Enveloped in the protection of his anonymity, John made his way to the tumbling water of the ornate fountains and snatched the nearest sheet of sodden paper from the water.

The paper wrapped around his gloved hand, making it difficult to make out the faded words on the page. Doing his best not to destroy the sheet as he unfolded it, the paper disintegrated in his hands. Overcome with frustration, John rolled the sodden sheet into a ball and hurled it back into the fountain.

'You should hide better than this.' Kimberley's familiar voice hushed from behind.

Rounding on her, Kimberley jumped back in surprise at John's reaction. There was no warmth in his posture, in fact, as he turned to face her John clenched his fist and fought to hold back the feeling of betrayal that washed over him.

'What were you doing with *her*?' John snarled through gritted teeth.

'I beg your pardon!'

'Diana, what were you doing meeting her here?'

'We should get away from here, I don't suppose she's gone that far. She could even be watching.'

'Let her watch!' John snapped. 'Whatever you have planned for me, whatever trap you pair ha concocted may as well happen now.'

'What are you talking about?'

'Don't push me.' John warned as he clenched his fists by his side. 'I'll fight every one that she sends at me. I just expected more from you.'

'John, I...'

'I'm not John to you, not anymore.' Despite his best attempts to hide it, there was an element of hurt in his voice as he dug his fingers into his palms.

'Please.' Kimberley pleaded, and took a step forward as John's attention moved away from her.

It was an early sign in his peripheral vision, a simple movement that seemed out of place against the world surrounding them. Having been so transfixed on Kimberley, his senses had focussed on her and given the approaching Revenants the concealment for their approach. Cursing himself for being lulled into Kimberley's presence, he pushed past her without a word and moved to meet the Revenants.

'It was always going to be easy enough to dangle her like bait.' One creature snarled as it came to stop a few metres away from John. 'For all your elusiveness, this almost seemed too easy.'

Joined by three others, John took in the measure of each of his opponents. It took little to realise this would be far from a fair fight. Removing the escrima sticks from his back, John chanced a glance back at Kimberley and offered her one last word.

'Pity my foolishness for trusting you.'

Offering no response, Kimberley turned and fled, disappearing amongst the sea of Londoners going about their daily business, oblivious to the shrouded fight that was about to take place in the iconic square.

'I take it there's no chance you'll simply surrender to your fate?'

'What do you think?' John replied, testing the weapons in each hand as he spoke. 'You're welcome to try to take me in.'

'Why do you think there are five of us?'

'Five?'

Cursing himself for a second time, John dodged to the side as the fifth Revenant crashed to the ground where he had been standing. Wasting no time in a counter-attack, John swiped the escrima stick through the air and heard the satisfying *crunch* as the wooden weapon smashed into the side of the demon Revenant's head, sending it crashing to the ground. Making sure his feet were grounded, John dropped low before launching forward towards the remaining demons in the hope he could seize the advantage.

Knowing the square was hardly the place for this fight, John took hold of the nearest creature and launched himself up towards the church spire that sat beside the National Gallery. Crashing into the tower, John and the Revenant tumbled down onto the rooftop below, closely followed by the four other creatures. Glad to be free of the meandering people, John shrugged off the shroud of his anonymity and allowed their raised position and cover of the building's shadows to keep them from view.

Dropping to his knee, John pinned the Revenant to the ground and opened his palm above the creature's head. Pinning it down, John ignored the clawing fingers that dragged down his coat and manifested the familiar swirling smoke in front of his hand. Not even wasting a second to share any words with the Revenant, John pressed the swirling smoke onto the Revenant's face and watched as the creature's head was stripped of flesh, features and skin until only the skull remained. With one last push of effort, John pressed the smoke to the ground, leaving nothing but a void where the Revenant's terrified head had been.

Satisfied the creature had been despatched, John extinguished the vortex of smoke and turned to face the remaining Revenants.

'As I was saying, the *four* of you can try to take me in, if you like.'

Knowing they would not back down, John smiled beneath the plague doctor mask and waited for them to attack.

3

UNSEEN BATTLES

John launched into the air at the first sign of movement from the Revenants. Making full use of his powers, he propelled towards the wall of the church spire and propelled himself off it and down towards his opponents. Rotating in the air, John crashed down onto the nearest of theRrevenants and wrapped the escrima stack around its neck. Pulling hard, the creature crashed to the floor with its head facing back away from its body. Stamping on the demon's chest, John was about to move when the second Revenant crashed into him.

Caught off-guard, the demon's weight threw him to the building's edge. With only a low edging, John's torso was pressed back over the edge as the others moved to join him. Fighting against the creature's strength and weight, John made a choice and launched the pair of them up and over the edge of the building. Allowing gravity to take its control over their decent, John positioned himself on top of the Revenant as they crashed into the pavement beside the church.

Cursing the fact he was visible, their landing was met with screams and panic from the pedestrians in the street. Seeing the crumpled mess of the Revenant beneath him, John rolled away and rose to his feet. Looking up, his heart sank as the others launched from the rooftop.

'Run.' John snarled at a dumbstruck bystander who held their phone out to record him.

Seeing the young man staring dumbfounded while fumbling with the phone, John knocked the device from his hand with the escrima stick.

'Hey!'

'You'd better run, this won't be pretty.' Before the young man could offer any further protest, John turned away and lurched towards the Revenants and their fight resumed.

Outnumbered, John had his work cut out to keep the four of them at bay. The two creatures he had taken out of commission were now thrashing around, attempting to contain him. Dragging its shattered legs behind it, the Revenant he had used to soften his landing now hoisted its way across the cobbled pavement, grasping for his legs at every opportunity. The other three were on their feet but of them, one of them fought with its head facing backwards and the bones protruding from its neck where John had snapped its spine.

Knowing they would draw attention, John had no chance to reclaim his anonymity as one Revenant slammed a heavy fist into the side of his head. Seeing stars, John fought to steady his spinning head as a second blow crashed into his chin. The power of the attack lifted him from the floor and sent him crashing into a telephone kiosk at the roadside. Sending glass splintering in all directions, John dropped to his knees and glared through the plague doctor mask.

Shaking the glass from his coat, John felt a tug at his shoulder and reached back to find a shard of glass protruding from the torn leather. Scrambling to prize it free from his flesh, John gripped the glass and ripped it out as the nearest Revenant attacked. Using the glass as a makeshift weapon, John dragged it across the Revenant's neck, leaving a deep gouge from one side to the other.

Not severing the demon's head completely, John delivered a return uppercut and heard the sickening sound as the remaining flesh tore with the power of his blow. Moving with astonishing speed, John dragged his hand through the air as the severed head tumbled to the ground and left a trail of black smoke in its wake. As the head disintegrated, John turned his attention back to the remaining two creatures.

He was at a loss in full view of the public. Knowing he was compromising everything about his shrouded existence, John pressed his hand against the motionless torso, causing it to shudder and disintegrate as its head had done. Content he was leaving nothing behind of the despatched Revenant, John turned towards the wall of the adjacent building and ran *up* the frontage of the structure. Moving with as much speed as he could muster, John reached the top and launched himself up and over onto the rooftop, and disappeared from view.

Dazed from the attacks, stars still dancing in his vision, John stumbled across the rooftop and leapt across to the next building as he heard the shrill cries of his hunters somewhere behind him. Feeling his feet go from beneath him, John could not stop his fall as he crashed into the fire escape and tumbled down into the scaffolding that covered the far side.

Bouncing off the wooden planks, John scrambled to grab the slippery poles as he crashed down the various levels until he caught himself halfway to the ground. Dangling by one arm, John swung himself out and landed on the level below, coming to rest against the pale facade of the building. Ripping the Moon-Blade from his back, John admired the golden decorations as he heard footsteps on the wood above.

'Give me a break.' John groaned as he rose to his feet and looked up to the sounds above.

Hearing the hunting Revenant's tracing the path of his escape, John jumped up and took hold of the support bars beneath the wooden planks of the level above. Pulling himself up, pressing his back against the wood, John kept himself out of view and waited for his hunters to move closer. Knowing his hiding place was not ideal, John waited before one of the Revenants dropped to the platform below.

Unwilling to waste the advantage, John dropped and as he did, sliced the crescent Moon-Blade through the air. Feeling the resistance as the hooked blade dug into the demon's skull, John smiled beneath the mask as he sliced the top third of the creature's skull. Hearing the sickening sound of the dead flesh and bone dropping at his feet, John jumped back and swiped the blade through the air as the Revenant turned to face him.

Watching the blade dig into the flesh on the side of his neck, John severed the creature's head in one swift movement. Knowing the creature was done, John wasted no time disposing of the body as he launched himself over the protective barrier and down to the street below. Knowing the Revenants would likely see him, John disappeared into the flow of pedestrians as his opponents scanned for him.

Grateful to have disappeared unseen by his pursuers, John felt his mind racing with a cascade of thoughts and concerns. The fact the Revenants had found him, filled him with a raging anger at Kimberley's betrayal. John once again navigated his way through the underground system until he found himself back at the forgotten Victorian underground station nestled between the modern lines of the underground. Surrounded by the crackle and rumble of modern life, there was a feeling of familiarity and comfort in the old design of the station.

'Bitch!' John screamed as he tore the mask from his face and tossed it onto a dusty bench. 'How could I have been so stupid?'

Reaching an old carriage that balanced against the wall of the station, John hoisted himself up the steps and disappeared within the shadows of the old carriage. Grateful for the anonymity, John set about removing his coat and admiring the injuries that covered his body. Ignoring the fact they were dead, when the undead fight, they could still leave marks on their opponents. Whatever dark magic bore the life from their silent hearts and lifeless bodies, allowed the marks of one against the other as a reminder of their precarious perch on the balance-beam between life and death.

Admiring the jagged wounds in his reflection, John scoffed at his reflection in the cracked glass.

'You've let her go again?' Death's voice hissed in the air and, as he looked around, John saw no sign of Azrael. 'You seem incapable of keeping her close by your side.'

'She wasn't who, or what, she would have had me believe.' John retorted as he turned his attention back to the broken mirror.

Despite being alone in the carriage, John could see Azrael in the cracked mirror reflection. Not giving Death the pleasure of seeing him search the carriage again, John locked his gaze on the robed visage of Death and waited.

'Didn't I bless you my sight to see beyond the exterior of the living?'

'You cursed me with that, yes!'

'Maybe I should come back when you remind me less of a moody adolescent?' Turning his back on John, Death made to leave.

'Wait!' John interjected with haste. 'You can't blame me for being slightly pissed. You only ever appear to taunt me with silly riddles or tasks like some amused parent-figure. Yet the times I need you, you hide in the shadows in silence.'

John was fighting to keep his tone calm as Azrael watched him through the broken mirror. Still keeping the heavy hood up and over his head, John could see nothing of Azraels face and could only stare into the dark shadows wondering whether the face beneath was as he remembered, a discoloured skull or else the familiar features of the face Azrael had often presented.

'My silence was your choice.' Azrael replied as he walked *out* of the mirror to stand in front of John. 'You are the one who severed yourself from me.'

'You didn't honour your promise.'

'As you didn't honour your oath!' Azrael snapped as he ripped back the hood.

Rather than allow the skin to cover the cream skull, Azrael kept his appearance as that of Death most recognisable to the world. Dressed in the heavy black robes, he appeared to almost float around John as he explored the length of the listing carriage.

'I did everything you asked of me.' John bit as he turned to face Azrael.

'Did you?'

'Do you have any idea how hard it is to keep your identity when you're surrounded by everyone else's thoughts?'

'Of course I do!' Azrael tilted his head to one side as he spoke. 'Get rid of the foolish notion you're the only one to dance this line, and please stop playing the victim. I expected more when I recruited you as my hand.'

'You made me the bloody victim.'

'You did that yourself.' Azrael barked, as he moved to tower over John. 'You gave the old warden the means to restrain you in that hospital. You willingly surrendered everything I gave you to fulfill your role as my sentinel amongst the living. Why?'

'I had no purpose. You left me alone.'

'It was not my place to interfere with your oath.'

'Stop speaking in riddles.' John lurched forward but stumbled as Azrael easily stepped aside.

'When you surrendered in that hospital, giving them the very tools to break the connection to your powers, you silenced our connection. Even if you thought your oath was complete, why would you give yourself up like that?'

'Because I was alone.' John sighed, dropping onto the moth-eaten seat. 'I felt lost and yet so consumed by the world, it felt like the only way to stop everything scratching inside my head.'

'It was a foolish choice.' Azrael was quick to soften the blow of his words. 'But I can understand why you did it.'

'I always believed they would let me free if you ever returned.'

'It was not my return you were waiting for.'

'The Ripper?'

'No.'

'Then who?'

'I would have thought that was obvious by now.'

'You're going to have to spell it out to me.'

'Your blindness to the details astounds me sometimes.' Azrael groaned as he stalked back towards the broken mirror. 'You are right. She isn't who or what you believe she is.'

Before he could offer any more questions, Azrael disappeared and John was once again alone inside the antique train carriage. Throwing his head back, John looked to the ceiling and watched a large spider make short work of enveloping a fly that had been caught in its web. Feeling an element of sympathy for both the spider and the fly, John closed his eyes and tried to make sense of Azrael's cryptic words.

4

———◆———

THE BURNT JEWEL

T he crimson crystal heart sat motionless atop the stone coffin in the crypt. As the shadows cast by the flickering candles danced on the stone lid, there was no sign the heart had ever lived. Having been recovered from the Zissuru, the heart of The Ripper was now nothing more than a relic and reminder of the darkness that the Raven had extinguished.

'We have tossed a snowball into the hill. The speed at which it gathers momentum is now out of our control.' Qamar sighed as he sat in front of the smouldering fireplace.

'Fate will make that decision.' Diana replied as she moved to the stone coffin to admire the shimmering heart. 'For what it's worth, you made the right choice.'

'Time will tell.'

'When do we move him?' Diana rested her thin fingers on the cold stone and closed her eyes for a moment.

Lost in her own thoughts, Diana did not hear Qamar's answer as she tried to feel the power contained within the stone coffin. The Society had retrieved The Ripper's remains from the

Zissuru and housed it in the secret crypt for almost a decade and still she longed to look inside. Having been nothing more than an ornament and reminder of the agreements made between the Society and the dark creatures of Sub Terra. Pressing her hand hard against the smooth stone, Diana found herself holding her breath, waiting to hear the voice from within.

'Compose yourself,' Qamar snapped as the flames spluttered in the fireplace. 'She's here.'

Opening her eyes, Diana removed her hand from the coffin and moved across the crypt to Qamar as the fireplace exploded into a fountain of flames. Unflinching, Qamar watched as the fire consumed the entire fireplace, tendrils flicking out towards him, but staying just out of reach. As Diana arrived behind her own chair, a silhouette appeared in the fire and as the flames subsided, they looked at a woman standing in front of them.

Dressed in a one-piece catsuit, her dark skin complimented the leather perfectly. Feline in her movement, she pulled her hair back over her face and took a moment to savour her arrival. Once all the flames had disappeared back into the smouldering logs behind her, she turned her attention to Diana and Qamar.

'I have never liked the means of passing into your realm that forces me to remain hidden.' There was something sinister in her voice, an almost reptilian hiss to her words as she stepped out of the fireplace. 'Diana, Qamar!'

'Amber.'

Stepping into the crypt, the shadows seemed to retract away from the new arrival. Having journeyed from the realm beyond life, Amber was familiar with the crypt and the Full Moon Society members stood before her. As a Dark Angel and messenger of Sub Terra, it had been her skills and prowess that had brokered the agreement with the Society to secure passage for her demons into the living realm. Despite the transition of leaders within the Society, Amber looked the same then as she had when the pact had been made, a fact not lost on either Diana or Qamar. Scanning the room, Amber's attention fell to the crimson crystal heart atop the stone coffin.

'I trust my Ripper's sacrifice was fruitful?' Stalking across the crypt, Amber snatched the heart from the lid and admired the geometric sides of the crystal.

'Everything is in motion.'

'You have Death's Hand?' Amber quizzed as she admired her reflection in the faces of the heart.

'Not yet.' Qamar offered as Amber snatched her attention to him.

'But your Ripper was the catalyst we needed, coupled with the woman, that rekindled his flame.'

'I don't want this to be another waste of a descended soul.' Amber hissed as she tossed the heart to Qamar. 'I won't be sending another of my demons to die on empty promises of success.'

'The prophecy will be fulfilled,' Diana interjected and moved towards Amber despite Qamar's attempts to hold her back. 'We have as much at stake her as you do.'

'Really?'

Amber moved with surprising speed as she closed Diana down and pressed the blade of a concealed dagger against her throat. Faces almost touching, Diana stared into Diana's eyes, who remained defiant and unblinking as she looked at the Dark Angel. Qamar could only watch in silence as the two women stared at one another, almost intimately. After a long moment, Amber removed the dagger from Diana's throat and gingerly brushed her fingers across the other woman's cheek.

'You're hiding a lot of fear.' Amber warned as she stalked back to the coffin. 'I can smell it on the both of you. No matter how much you try to hide it, I can almost taste it in this pathetic relic to an order that once held my respect.'

'How dare you?' Qamar boomed as he stalked past Diana and pressed the Ripper's heart into her hands as he passed. 'We represent the Full Moon Society. If it wasn't for us, you wouldn't be able to be stand here now.'

'You represent the respectable Society I made our pact with. What you represent is a mere shadow of what once was. Do not overestimate your position.'

'And don't forget that you need us.'

Qamar's brashness even caught Diana by surprise as she watched him hold himself in front of Amber. Admiring the Dark Angel from afar, Diana turned her attention to the crystal heart in her hand. Feeling a curious heat in her hand, she was about to speak when the heart erupted into flames. Recoiling from the burning heart, Diana dropped it to the ground at her feet.

All eyes fell to the burning heart on the ground. Grateful for the distraction, Qamar moved close as the flames changed through the spectrum of colours until it settled on a gloriously vibrant green light that rose into the air between them. Filling the air with a sound like crickets in the night, it crescendoed so loud both Diana and Qamar clamped their hands over their ears.

Without warning, the crypt was filled with a blinding light and as it dissipated, silence had once again descended and the heart was no longer ablaze. Instead of the shimmering crimson faces, the heart was now charred and blackened and it was Amber who broke the eerie silence that hung in the room.

'It would appear you were right.' Amber oozed as she looked at Diana. 'The prophecy shall be fulfilled.'

'A burnt jewel.' Diana gasped as she bent down and tapped the heart to check if it was still hot to the touch.

'A hell demons throne.' Qamar added.

'Both twins will meet a fight.' Amber finished as she returned to the fireplace. 'My Ripper's sacrifice was the second catalyst. Pray your placement of the woman has done enough to awaken the powers inside the Raven.'

Disappearing once back in the fireplace, Qamar and Diana were once again alone in the crypt. Picking up the charred heart, Diana returned it to its resting place atop the coffin before stalking out of the crypt. Only once she was out of view, no longer observed by Qamar, Diana allowed her emotions to show. Having seen the display of supernatural power, her body shook and her eyes filled with tears.

For so long she had yearned to earn the respect, and trust, of Amber, and now it finally appeared to be happening. As one of the most senior members of the Society, she had not fought her way through the ranks without confrontation and yet, standing in front of Amber, she felt it had all been nothing compared to standing before the Dark Angel. As Diana had felt the cold metal press against her throat, she knew how delicately her life hung in the balance. resting herself against the stone wall outside the crypt, Diana couldn't help but wonder what would have happened if the heart had not burst into flames.

Not wanting to be caught in a state of emotion, Diana moved along the subterranean corridor until she reached the stairs leading back up to the streets of London. As she made it halfway up the winding staircase, the ringing of her phone filled the air. Jumping on the step, Diana cursed as she ripped the phone from her pocket and checked the display. Not recognising the number, she almost dismissed the call, but changed her mind and answered it.

'Who is this?'

'You put me there on purpose, didn't you?' Kimberley barely controlled the anger in her voice. 'You just wanted John to see me, didn't you?'

'I knew he would be somewhere nearby.' Diana composed herself as she emerged from the anonymous doorway, made her way across an empty courtyard before merging with the flow of Londoners along the banks of the Thames.

'I'm not a pawn in your ridiculous games.'

'That's exactly what you are.' Diana spat as she walked. 'You forgot who it was that put you in the room with John.'

'Was that for a reason too?'

'It's taken you this long to realise?' Diana scoffed. 'Perhaps your reputation as an astute and clever young student was over-played by your tutor.'

'I'm done with you.' Kimberley snapped. 'I won't be a pawn in your games anymore.'

'That's fine. You have outlived your use, anyway.'

Ending the call, Diana slipped the phone back into her pocket and continued along the path alongside the Thames. Smiling to herself, she paid no attention to the world around her. Disappearing into the crowds, she never saw Kimberley as she tossed the phone she had used to call Diana into the churning water of the river. Hidden from the flow of people, Kimberley had known where Diana would emerge, having followed her after their meeting in Trafalgar Square.

She had not known what would come from the call, more than anything she wanted to get a feel for Diana's intentions towards her. The coldness of the warden's replies told her she was no great concern to Diana. Knowing that was more of a concern than if Diana had told her she wanted her removed from the dance she was involved in. Dismissing Kimberley's presence meant she was no longer considered a threat or even of consequence, which she realised meant she was disposable.

'Unnerving isn't it?'

Kimberley yelped as she turned at the sound of John's voice behind her. Shocked to find the space behind her empty, it wasn't until she looked up that she found him balanced on the fire escape of the building she had used to shadow herself in. Unable to see his face behind the plague doctor mask, Kimberley longed to see any emotion on his face, any sign of what he was thinking, but knew better than to push.

'I'm not part of this.'

'You are very much a part of this.' John hissed from behind the mask. 'Whether you know it, I'm yet to decide.'

'None of this was my doing.' Kimberley pleaded as she inched further into the secluded alleyway. 'They've played me as much as they've played you.'

'You'll forgive me if I find that hard to believe.'

'You obviously doubt yourself enough to be here now.' Kimberley raised an eyebrow and foolishly offered her open hands to him. 'Do what you want with me, but I'm only part of this because of you.'

'Won't they protect you?' John motioned with his mask towards the anonymous door on the far side of the river. 'Or have they cast you to the wolves?'

'I expect they'll send one of those Revenant things to kill me soon enough.'

'Death seems to believe you're important to me.'

'Am I?'

'That remains to be seen.' John dropped to stand in front of her. 'While it remains a possibility, I won't leave you to the wolves.'

'Thank you.' John silenced her with a raised hand.

'Save your thanks. This is more about me finding out the bloody mess that surrounds you than protecting you. While our fates are entwined, I'll offer you sanctuary.'

Not giving her a chance to reply, John turned his back and stalked along the alleyway. Not offering her any more of an invitation, John knew she would follow. Leaving the bustling capital behind them, John guided her to the hidden sanctuary he had found in the long forgotten subterranean labyrinths of London's underground network.

5

REVELATIONS

Kimberley walked around the old station, aware that John was watching from the shadows high above. Having taken his perch on the metal beams, he had not spoken to her since they had emerged into the dusty station.

'You can't hide from her forever.' Azrael's voice hushed from the shadows at his side. 'You aren't going to learn anything by sulking like a teenager.'

'Can't you shut up?' John hissed.

'So now, after all your complaining, you want me to be silent again?' Azrael's voice was filled with mockery. 'So be it.'

Hearing a *pop* in the air, John knew Azrael was making a point. Frustrated beyond belief, John could not focus on the bigger picture as his mind kept wandering back to the young woman below as she explored the abandoned station. Even from his vantage point, John could see the tiredness and confusion on her face. Whether it was a ruse or façade, John was yet to work out. Although the matter of the Revenant's increased attention and drive to detain him filled him with concern.

Deciding, John dropped from the metal girder and landed on the dusty platform ahead of Kimberley. Although she spoke, John paid no attention to her words and stalked towards her. Offering her no choice, John ripped the glove from his hand and pressed his palm against her forehead. The moment their skin touched, John dragged them both from the sanctuary of his hideaway and into a place Kimberley had never explored before.

Unwilling to take Kimberley into his own memories, John took them into the space between consciousness and memories. Surrounded by the sounds of water, he allowed a fantastic world to take shape around them.

'Where is this place?' Kimberley gasped as she drank in their surroundings.

Revelling in the confusion, John moved to the edge of the floating platform and looked out at the vast world of impossibility that surrounded them. The world was a fusion of past and present, with elements of industrialisation and nature fused together in symbiosis. Plumes of jet-black smoke tumbled from chimneys while enormous cogs protruded from the floating patches of land that flew in the air, untouched by gravity. It was difficult to work out which way was up, as each pod of land and industrialisation sat at an odd angle from the next. Beyond all realm of possibility, John watched a cascade of water from a factory overspill pipe pour upwards, towards the sky.

'This is the junction we always pass through when I take you into my mind.' John soothed as he admired the curious and somewhat broken landscape. 'You've never seen it before because it is nothing more than a launchpad into whatever moment in time I intended you to see.'

'So what is different now?' Kimberley snapped from across the narrow piece of floating land. 'Why have we stopped here this time? I don't suspect it would be by chance.'

'Ever astute!' John bit, his usual playful demeanour no longer anywhere to be seen.

'Just ask.' Kimberley yelled as a piece of land tumbled head over tails above them. 'I know you think I'm with them, but I'm not! What would I have to gain from any of this?'

'You tell me.' John fought to contain his anger. 'I know where you went when the Ripper locked you in our memories.'

'Your grave?'

'Exactly.' The look of confusion was blatantly obvious on Kimberley's face, a fact that riled John all the more as he glared at her. 'How could you have even known of that place.'

'Because it was in your bloody memories. You're the one who put me there, more than once.'

'But I never took you to that place. I never gave you access to that place.'

'So how did I find myself there, talking to that woman who sent me to find you with the Ripper?'

'What woman?'

'I'm not sure. She told me to follow your heart, and that's how I found you.' Kimberley tried to replay the memory in her mind and suddenly the surrounding skies darkened a little. 'If it wasn't for me, the Ripper could have defeated you. I stopped it.'

'I can't help but feel it was another ruse to lull me into feeling secure with you.'

'Have I ever given you any reason to disbelieve me?'

'Many!'

'Such as?'

'Why did you seek me out when I recovered the texts from the Society? Why did you seek my grave? How did you find your way through my memories? Why were you even at the hospital in the first place?'

John's rage boiled over as he closed her down. In one swift move, John hoisted Kimberley into the air and dangled her over the edge of the platform. With nothing beneath her feet, he saw the panic in Kimberley's eyes as she grasped onto his arm and fought to find the ground.

'What are you doing?' Her voice was overcome with panic.

'I need to know what part you're playing.' John stared into her eyes as the plague doctor mask grew over his face. 'And if you won't tell me, then you will *show* me.'

Shifting his weight forward, both of them tumbled over the edge of the platform and the air was immediately filled with the sound of Kimberley's panicked screams. Despite her fear, their fall was over in a matter of seconds as a darkness enveloped them and the now familiar view Victorian London took shape around them. Landing roughly on the cobbled pavement, Kimberley crashed to the ground while John remained upright. Leaving her to right herself, John took in their new surroundings.

'How would you know about this place?' John hissed from behind the Raven's mask.

'I don't even know where this place is.' Kimberley denied as she dusted herself off. 'I've never been here...wait.'

John snatched his attention towards Kimberley as she looked around at the Victorian street. Surrounded by townhouses, this could have been any street in London, and yet it was much more than that to John. Looking beyond Kimberley, his gaze fell on an all too familiar red door that sat at the top of a steep flight of steps. As if sensing his attention, the door opened and, before he could see who emerged, he turned away and looked in the opposite direction.

'Wait, what?' John hissed as he fought to compose himself.

'I know this place, but that can't be possible.'

'Explain.'

'This street, I recognise it from a photo my mother has in her bedroom.'

'Think about it.' John commanded through gritted teeth. 'Think about that photo and bring it here.'

'What do you mean?'

'Think of the bloody picture.' John yelled, making Kimberley jump where she stood.

Keeping his back to the red-door house, John waited for the inevitable gasp of surprise as the photograph manifested itself in Kimberley's hands as if by magic. Hearing her sharp intake of breath, John steeled himself and turned around to face her. Not allowing his eyes to wander to the figure walking along the street away from them, John moved to Kimberley and snatched the picture from her grasp. Turning it to face him, John could line the photograph up against the backdrop of the street, including the red-door house. The photograph was an old sepia image of the very street they were standing in, faded and dogeared, John felt a lump in his throat as he looked at the woman and young boy's face in the photo.

'I can't believe I didn't recognise her.' Kimberley sighed. 'That's the woman who spoke to me at your grave.'

'How do you know her?'

'Why? Who is she to you?'

'I asked first.' John replied, his voice softening just enough to betray the drop in his defences, as the mask faded from his face.

'My mother always kept that photograph on her bedside table.' Kimberley explained as the mask faded from John's face. 'She told me it was the only surviving photograph after everything else was lost in a house fire.'

'But who are they to you?' John's cold expression was no longer there, replaced now with a furrowed brow and deep sadness in his eyes. 'Why would your mother have this photo?'

'Because that was her grandad there.'

Kimberley pointed to the young boy in the photograph. Dressed in traditional Victorian attire, the boy had a head of neatly combed hair and looked no older than six or seven years old. His mother, dressed in a long dress, offered no smile to the unseen camera, a fact that had always unnerved Kimberley since she had been a child.

'That can't be true.' John returned his attention to Kimberley.

'I always found it weird how sad they looked.' Kimberley continued, ignoring John's gaze. 'My family has never been close. Although he was an only child, my grandma was one of five and my mum has two brothers. His name was...'

'Alexander.'

'How do you know that?'

Dropping the photograph, John pushed past Kimberley and stalked along the street towards the house with the red door. Pausing at the bottom of the steps, John heard Kimberley moving to join him and quickly made his way up to the door. As he reached the top step, the door opened and John stopped dead in his tracks. Just inside the doorway stood the young boy from the photograph. Not daring to disrupt the memory, John stepped aside as the boy leapt down the stairs and looked away up the street.

'Mum?' The young boy's voice echoed in the air, and John tensed at the sound of his voice.

As Kimberley joined him at the top of the stairs, they watched as the woman from the photograph joined the young boy. Moving along the street, they both realised this was the moment they had taken the photo and could only watch as the photographer set his equipment up on the side of the cobbled road. Sensing

John's unease at what was happening, Kimberley tentatively pressed to find out what this all meant to him.

'Azrael said I was being blind to the most obvious things that were right in front of me.' John mused as he looked at Kimberley. 'My only worry is, if you knew, then you are deeper entrenched with the Full Moon Society than I had feared.

'Knew what?'

'Alexander was my son.' John declared, paying careful attention to Kimberley's reaction. 'He was only a baby when I died, but I watched him grow from the shadows.'

'Your son?' Kimberley gasped, computing the gravity of John's declaration. 'But that would mean...'

Allowing her to trail off, it satisfied John her response was genuine. The sudden loss of colour from her face and the uncontrollable tremble in her body told him as much. The realisation was not lost on him either, their paths crossing could not have been by chance and more than anything he needed to know to what end they had manipulated Kimberley into the position she was now in.

'That means, we...' her voice trailed off. '...you're my...'

'It means we are of the same blood. Whatever way you look at it, something, or someone, destined our paths to cross at some point. But I suspect the Society have been long aware of this, and you were positioned in front of me for a reason I'm yet to understand.'

'I need to get out of here.' Reminiscent of the panic he had seen when he had first taken her into his memories, John released her from the memory and the world collapsed, giving way to the subterranean station.

Pulling away from him, Kimberley's eyes were wide as she fought to calm her racing breaths. Consumed by panic, John knew it was best to leave her be and stood aside as she sprinted along the platform away from him.

'You knew?' John asked the space by his side.

'I knew.'

'And you never saw fit to tell me?'

'No.'

'Curse you.' John hissed. 'You really are a cold bastard.'

Stalking in the opposite direction as Kimberley, it was not only her that needed time to process the gravity of what they had just discovered.

6

PICKING UP THE PIECES

By the time John found Kimberley, she was sitting at the end of the collapsed tunnel beyond the abandoned platform. With her back against the piles of stones and twisted metal, she hugged her knees and paid him no attention as his footsteps echoed down the tunnel towards her. Knowing she would be reeling from the revelation, much as he was, John had given her as much time as he could, before disturbing her.

'You should eat something.' John declared as he dropped a bag by Kimberley's side.

'I'm not hungry.'

'Regardless, you need food.' John argued as he pulled a large piece of masonry from the pile to use as a seat. 'And besides, we need to talk.'

'I'm not in the mood for talking.' Kimberley snapped as she rummaged through the bag despite herself.

'Fine.' John sighed as he pulled a file from inside his coat and threw it at her feet. 'But you'll want to read through those. When you've done, I'll be in the carriage.'

Leaving her alone, John disappeared back towards the platform. Seeing his silhouette disappear out of the tunnel's opening, Kimberley finally allowed her attention to fall to the scattered paperwork on the old track. Opening the sandwich from the bag, Kimberley set about collecting the paperwork together and laying it out in front of her.

'What is this?' She mused as she realised how hungry she was.

Chewing the sandwich with haste, Kimberley almost choked on the stale bread as she realised the file's content and focus was on her. Seeing photographs of her in various familiar places it surprised her to see photographs going back to her university days. Seeing her own past in the collection of images, she moved her attention to the array of printed sheets that accompanied the photos. Struggling to see the details in the light, Kimberley collected everything together and made her way back towards the main platform, but only after she had finished the contents of the food bag John had given her.

'Took you longer than expected.' John mused as Kimberley clambered into the listing carriage.

'What's all this about?' Kimberley hushed as she began laying the contents of the file across the makeshift table fashioned between the old seats. 'Where did you get this?'

'The same guy who I took the parchment from.' John offered a wry smile as he explained. 'You'd be surprise how easy it was while you were preoccupied.'

'Why did he have this?' Kimberley snatched up one photograph that showed her sat in a lecture, studiously making notes. 'This is from my first year at uni. That's six years ago.'

'They've been watching you for that long. Longer even.'

'Why?'

'Because of who you are to me.' John sighed as he joined her at the makeshift table. 'They've clearly known for a lot longer than we have.'

'But we are talking almost a decade.' Kimberley muttered as she laid out the photos in some sort of timeline as she remembered it. 'How can they have even been watching me for that long? I didn't even know about you back then.'

'I have a feeling they've controlled everything about your past.' John explained as he scanned the images. 'They've clearly known about your bloodline and manipulated you into a position where our paths would cross.'

'That's impossible. You're not telling me a woman I met only a few weeks ago has somehow controlled that everything I've ever done?'

'I'm saying exactly that.' John sighed as he dropped onto a seat. 'Whether it was Diana or others in the Society, they've played you like a chesspiece it would seem.'

'To what end?' John struggled to find his voice to answer. Avoiding her gaze, he kept his attention on the pile of paperwork. 'What aren't you telling me?'

'When I surrendered to the old warden, I gave them the dampening bracelets.'

'Yes, to contain your power.'

'It did more than that.' John continued. 'The longer they stayed on, the more distant I moved from my connection to the afterlife.'

'But it was always there.' Kimberley pressed as she moved to sit opposite him.

'I know it was there, but sometimes they tried to tease my powers back.'

'Why would they do that?' She longed to make eye contact, to see the hidden emotion, but John kept his gaze directed at the dusty floor. 'Wouldn't it be dangerous to let you have them back? Look what happened when I removed the bracelets.'

'And that is the interesting thing. Every other time they removed them, I felt no connection to Azrael.' John's voice was barely above a whisper. 'There was a room in the bowels of that bloody hospital where they would unbind me long enough to see if I could call back the Raven, and it never worked.'

'Did they ever explain why?'

'I suspected it was along the lines of some misguided idea that they wanted to control me, or take control of my powers. But now I'm not too sure.'

'So, what are you saying? They brought me back because I could make you work again?'

'Evidently, that was the case. The tests only began when Diana arrived. Before then, the old warden was happy to leave me be.'

'Did he know?'

'Of course he did! It took some convincing, but he was a good man. I trusted him.'

'Can you be sure he wasn't part of the Full Moon Society?' Kimberley pressed, seeing him tense at the question.

'Honestly, I won't ever know. But I choose to believe he was a good man.'

'That's good enough for me.' She offered him a feigned smile as he briefly looked up at her. 'So, when Diana arrived, that's when they started these experiments with you?'

'That's what tells me he wasn't from the Society.' John sighed as he rose to his feet. 'Once Diana arrived, the feeling was different.'

'But what difference would I make?'

'That's what I've been thinking about.' John turned to face the cracked mirror at the far end of the carriage. 'And despite his silence, I expect Azrael knows more than he would let on?'

'You've been doing so well to explain this by yourself.' Azrael replied as he materialised in the space between them and the broken mirror.

Kimberley immediately launched from her seat and backed away. Having seen Death in John's vision, it was not his appearance that frightened her, more the fact she could see them in her world, in the *real* world! Watching in disbelief, Kimberley dared not say a word as Azrael removed his mask and, much like she had seen in John's memory, the familiar face of Death grew over the exposed skull until he once again looked human.

'You have nothing to fear, Kimberley.' Azrael offered as he invited her to take her seat again. 'You aren't on my radar for any other reason than the unfortunate company you keep.'

'And the fact we are related?' Kimberley pressed as she tentatively sidled around the seat.

'Well, that too.' Azrael disarmed her with his charm. 'But that's a series of unfortunate events that could have been avoided.'

'Don't start making it all about me.' John snapped, feeling Azrael's attention. 'If you had honoured my oath, I could have been welcomed into whatever afterlife you had in store for me.'

'Well yes, but once you've fulfilled that oath, I'll gladly honour it.' Azrael jibed as he moved to join them at the makeshift table. 'The events in the Zassuru should remind you that things were not as complete as you thought.'

'But they are now!' John bit.

'But now you have a ward. Am I likely to grant you peace and freedom from your duty as a sentinel and protector, knowing you've exposed this poor soul to their attention?'

'Well,' John stammered to find the right words.

'Exactly!' Azrael rested his scythe against the side of listing carriage and snatched up one image from the table. 'The moment you surrendered yourself, you set these events in motion.'

'Can I ask something' Kimberley interrupted nervously.

'By all means.'

'I feel you know a lot more than you let on. I mean, you're Death, right? Surely you can just tell us what to do and we can both be free of this, mess?'

'It's not that simple.'

'It never is.' John interrupted. 'Always some catch or clause to make a simple task far more complicated than it needs to be.'

'You should be less dismissive of that fact. If it wasn't this way, you'd have died in Whitechapel.'

Azrael's declaration brought an uneasy silence to the carriage. Seeing the tension between the two of them, Kimberley was cautious to press, but knew she had to understand more about the complicated world John and Azrael occupied.

'What do you mean by that?' Kimberley finally asked, hoping to break the tension between the two men.

'There are rules that keep the balance between life and death.'

'It's not exactly working though, is it?' John snarled. 'I've only been back a short time and I can already see the balance isn't where it was when I left. Revenants walking the streets, demons feeding off the living.'

'There will always be sways either side of order, but the rules keep us from descending into chaos.' Azrael argued. 'You were employed as my hand to give me a presence beyond what I am permitted to do.'

'So I stand on the other side of balance?'

'You do, don't act so surprised. Your existence is necessary to make sure the pendulum doesn't sway in favour of the Dark Angel and creatures of Sub terra.'

'It seems they aren't playing by the same rules.'

'You're not in a position to make comment. The order would be maintained had you been in a position as my sentinel, not hiding in the shadows as a lab rat for the Full Moon Society.'

'What is their place in all this?' Kimberley asked, feeling the palpable tension between Azrael and John growing.

'They are the fools who believe they will be rewarded with immortality when the balance sways in favour of darkness and evil. They are corrupt individuals who would sell their souls to guarantee their own survival.' Azrael's words were laced with hatred, his tone betraying his feelings towards the Society. 'The Raven's sole responsibility was to curb and curtail the exploration of demons from Sub Terra. Your absence has allowed them to swell in numbers.'

'And what happens if you tell us everything, rather than leave us fumbling in the dark?'

'A betrayal of the ancient covenant between Ascent and Sub Terra will open the floodgates for the opposing side.'

'You're telling me the fact they are swelling in numbers means they are honouring this agreement? You're a bigger fool than I thought!'

'John, please.' Kimberley interjected. 'Nothing in this is as black and white as either of us would like to believe.'

'Don't tell me you're buying into this.'

'Don't tell me you're not!'

'The swell in their numbers is acceptable because they invite it. A loophole the Dark Angel Amber has always exploited for their own gain.'

'You mean because the Full Moon Society helps them and provides them a means to feed, it's not considered imbalance?' The disbelief was clear in her tone. 'Thats' ridiculous, they don't speak for all of humanity.'

'Regardless, an invitation to feed does not count.' Azrael silenced John with a stern glare as he offered a loud sigh. 'Bringing you two together has awoken the gifts I gave you when you became my hand, the same gifts you lost when you surrendered yourself.'

'To what end?' John barked, slamming his fist onto the makeshift table. 'Give us at least some idea where to start.'

'Now your paths have merged, you will find the greatest strength remaining together.' Azrael replaced the hood over his head and as the shadows swallowed his face, Kimberley saw the skin retract back behind the bones. 'Your fates are entwined with Diana and the Full Moon Society.'

'Is that it?' John snapped. 'Cryptic crap.'

'Heed the prophecy of the Society, it will give you guidance towards what is coming.'

'You know, don't you?' Kimberley pressed as Azrael moved back towards the broken mirror.

'No fate is sealed. My gift allows me to see the shapes and shadows of your futures.' As Azrael faded, he offered them one last thought. 'Heed the prophecy of the Society, understand their meaning and all will be revealed.'

As he disappeared, their attention fell to the mirror as the cracks somehow moved to spell out the prophecy.

A BURNT JEWEL
A HELL DEMONS THRONE
BOTH TWINS WILL MEET A FIGHT

7

— • —

BLOOD MOON

Qamar commanded the room as he sauntered out from behind a large curtain and took his place on the raised platform. Dressed in a curious ensemble, long draping robes and a black mask over the lower part of his face, he turned as Diana emerged to join him.

'Brothers and sisters,' Qamar announced, his voice echoing around the vast room. 'We gather to mark the beginning of the prophecy.'

The room was filled with a hundred or more robed figures, all with their faces disguised beneath a veil of muslin. They arranged the gathered audience in specific rows, the colours of their robes reflecting their place in the ranks starting with a garish green furthest back to a blood-red crimson for the front two rows. Qamar could have heard a pin drop in the room, and although he could not see them, he felt every pair of eyes beneath the veils watching him with unflinching attention.

'We stand gathered as one in the crypt of our founders. The Porta Inferni has not hosted the Full Moon Society in these numbers since we made the promise to the Dark Angel.' It was Diana who continued the ritualistic introduction. As she spoke, the gathered figures stamped their left feet in unison. Over the crescendo of stamps, Diana projected her voice with confidence. 'They have acknowledged our efforts.'

'The ritual shall begin.' Qamar boomed as he moved to stand in front of Diana.

Hiding her frustration, grateful for the mask covering her face, she could only watch as Qamar stole the attention of the now chanting crowd. Drowning out his words, Diana took the time to admire the simplicity of the Porta Inferni. Buried beneath London itself, they had protected the temple from curious eyes for centuries. Hidden in plain sight, the power of the Society had kept the land above the crypt protected from development or historical excavation.

Mastering the art of misdirection, it had been Qamar who had set about protecting the crypt. This gathering was the first time the Porta Inferni had seen anyone other than Diana, Qamar and Amber gathered beneath the inverted dome roof high above. Casting her attention to the ceiling, it still amazed Diana that the roof somehow remained in position rather than crumbling in a heap on the marble floor below. Bulging in the centre, the inverted dome had been hand painted with an intricate pattern of black and red that gave an illusion the ceiling was pulsing in the flickering firelight.

Opposite the bulbous dome, the gathered crowds were careful to avoid a metal grate in the centre of the floor. Crafted from polished gold, the grate shimmered in the light and only Diana and Qamar knew the demon's hole was positioned directly above the stone coffin that had been removed from the Zassuru. It was that coffin and the now burned crystal heart sitting atop it that was the focus of the impending ritual. As Qamar's words invoked a hushed silence among the gathered crowd, Diana returned her attention to the sea of concealed faces and cast aside her thoughts of what had passed to bring them to this moment.

'We stand together, formed of single mind to bring forth the powers that would normally be contained by fear.'

Turning to face her, Qamar locked gazes with Diana as he removed a small dagger from the belt of his robes. Similar to the moon blade, this was an intricate weapon, curved blade and gilded handle of which Diana had the same in her belt. Knowing his meaning, Diana retrieved her own and watched as the gathered worshipers did the same. Placing the weapon on their chest, hovering above where their heart would be, Qamar offered her a wink and turned back to face the crowd.

'Together, we make an oath of blood. Beneath the moon, in service to the Dark Angel, we secure our immortality by bringing life from death.'

As he spoke, a column rose from the floor in front of him. Etched from pale marble, the column appeared to be a pair of arms pressed together with the open hands forming a bowl at the top. Angled as they were, the space between the palms and arms pressed together made a natural channel that traveled down to the ground and the edge of the platform Qamar and Diana were standing on.

'Where once a single soul would seek to resurrect feed the shadows and, in so doing, sacrifice their life. Together, now we are many so that the blood sacrifice does not come at the expense of life.' Diana declared as she moved to stand beside Qamar and levelled her own blade to point at the nearest of the crimson-cloaked figures. 'Such is the strength of a Society of like minds that sees the truth and knows the injustice that keeps the shadows from finding their home.'

'We make our oath.' The chorus of voices declared as they raised their own blades to the sky. 'We spill our blood so that life may be born from the darkness.'

'Step forth and fulfill your promise.'

As both Diana and Qamar moved back from the marble column, the first of the robed figures moved to the platform. Silently, they ascended the steps to the column and held out their right hand above the open marble palms. Pressing the hooked blade of the knife against their palm, they deliberately drew the razor-sharp metal across their hand from top to bottom. Hearing the wince against the pain, Diana watched as the faceless figure turned their hand over and squeezed a fist, forcing a steady stream of blood to ooze into the smooth polished marble palms.

Diana could only watch as one by one the gathered figures repeated the same process. In blind obedience, they each scored their palm in the same manner and allowed their blood to flow into the cupped hands that waited to receive it. As the volume within the makeshift chalice reached its overflow point, the blood flowed down the gulley created by the carved arms and towards the floor. As her eyes traced the route of the blood as more and more flowed down the pale marble, Diana could see the outline of a crescent moon stretching from the platform, to finish at the gilded grate in the centre of the floor. The flowing blood stained the shimmering gold, and it amazed her to see how much blood had been sacrificed, and still less than half of the robed figures had made their offering.

'You see their obedience?' Qamar hushed in her ear. 'Never has the Society been so strong, amassed in such numbers. You have done this.'

'We, we have done this.' Diana replied, and she saw the pride in Qamar's eyes.

'Let them continue their offering. We should retire.'

'What of our sacrifice?' Diana protested as she saw the snaking line of devotees waiting their turn.

'Our sacrifice is on a different level.' Qamar declared as he turned back to the hanging curtain at the back of the platform. Our time will come, but this is not for us.'

Knowing she would follow, Qamar stalked away through the curtain without breaking pace. Casting her attention back to the obedient robed figures, spending more time than she should have admiring their sacrifice, Diana eventually followed through the curtain and descended the spiral staircase that was obscured from view. Knowing where it would lead, despite the lack of light, Diana knew the route well enough not to stumble or struggle on the spiralling steps. When she reached the bottom and pushed open the wooden door, she found herself once again in the crypt with Qamar stood before the fireplace and four Revenants on all fours in prayer beside the now bloodstained coffin passing the stream of sacrificial blood that poured in through the grate. Seeing the blood, Diana could not help but admire the sacrifice by their followers.

'The Dark Angel has confirmed, the ritual has begun.' The flames within the fireplace disappeared and Diana saw no sign of the Dark Angel Amber silhouetted by the dying fire. 'We have taken the first steps.'

'And what of the remaining sacrifice?' Diana pressed as she removed the black mask from her face and tasted the stale air of the crypt. 'When will that be required?'

'When the moment arises.' Qamar snapped.

'Are we any nearer?'

'You tell me. You were the last to speak with your pet. Did you learn anything from her?'

'It appears she has outlived her use.' Diana sighed as she slumped into one chair. 'The Revenants lost the Raven, and she appears to have disappeared.'

'If she is of no use, we could use her scent to find them both.' Qamar mused as he nudged the smouldering logs with his shoe. 'Unless you object?'

'Meaning?' Diana sensed the playful curiosity in Qamar's voice.

'You seem fond of her. If not, a little reluctant to see her use ended.'

Diana couldn't deny she had grown an almost motherly fondness towards Kimberley. The years of manipulation from the shadows had seen her watching over and directing the young woman along a path very similar to her own. Although Kimberley had never truly known the extent of Diana's control over her life, it had always been in the back of her mind that Kimberley could have been groomed towards the Society at the right moment. Seeing her allegiance swing towards John had been an unexpected turn of events and nothing short of a crippling disappointment.

'She has been integral to all of this for so long. I won't deny I wished more for her in the end.'

'Sentimentality, from you of all people?' Qamar jibed as she turned to face her. 'Not something I would have expected to see.'

'I stand by the choice to use her.'

'Oh, as do I.'

'I'm simply a little sad to see it be fruitless for her.'

'You seem like a disappointed mother.'

The words stung, and Diana struggled to hide her anger at Qamar's declaration. He knew her sacrifices of motherhood for the Full Moon Society and such a casual dismissal ignited the anger buried deep inside her. Quick to control herself, Diana returned the conversation to more palatable grounds.

'Bringing them together was always going to be a risk, for both of them.' Diana conceded as she sensed the four Revenants end their worship of the bloodstained coffin and turn their attention to her. 'I had hoped she would have awoken his powers and have moved on.'

'But their blood bond is stronger than you anticipated.' One Revenant hissed from behind. 'A common thing with you. Underestimating the Raven.'

'Not at all.' Diana dismissed with a wave of her hand. 'I suspect even John underestimated the disconnection provided by these bracelets. What I had hoped would be a simple spark through my methods at the hospital clearly needed more fuel than a human intervention.'

'We can find the woman.' The Revenant declared as its tongue tasted the air behind her, and despite herself, Diana tensed at the thought.

'The choice is yours, Diana.' Qamar offered, handing Kimberley's fate to her on purpose.

'You can sense her?'

'We can.' The Revenant declared as she turned to face them. 'She is shrouded in some ways, but unlike the Raven, she cannot hide completely.'

'Then use her to find him.' Diana sighed. 'We are too far along now to sacrifice our chance to fulfil the prophecy.'

Her attention fell to the bloodstained stone and the steady stream of blood that continued to dribble from the golden grate in the crypt's ceiling. Seeing the sinister look of excitement in the Revenant's lifeless eyes, she knew the fate she was securing for Kimberley. Despite her feelings, Diana knew it was the only way to bring about the prophecy and honour the legacy she had vowed to protect.

Hushing its commands to the other three Revenants, Diana watched as they left the crypt, leaving only the single demon standing in the doorway looking at her. As she met its gaze, Diana felt the unseen tendrils as the Revenant explored her consciousness. Tensing at the curious feeling, she composed herself as she heard the demonic creature's voice in her head, unheard by anyone but her.

'Your feelings for her tell me you would rather see her endure another fate.' The Revenant hissed inside her head. 'There is something inside you are not allowing yourself to see and feel. I will make her death swift.'

Offering the creature the slightest of nods, it turned and took its leave from the crypt. Feeling completely violated, the invisible touch inside her head still raw and tender, Diana dropped back into the seat and returned her attention to the fireplace. Looking beyond Qamar, she once again read the carved inscription of the prophecy etched into the stone.

'What did it say to you?' Qamar quizzed as he moved past Diana, placing his hand on her shoulder.

'He promised me a swift death for her.'

'Anything else?'

'No.' Lying, she kept her gaze fixed on the fireplace.

'Yu will find another pet project.' Qamar comforted as he squeezed her shoulder. 'When the ritual is complete and the promises honoured, you will have centuries to find a new daughter.'

Tensing, Diana felt the tears well in her eyes but fought to stop them from falling. Taking his leave, Qamar left her alone in the crypt, and as the door shut behind him, Diana breathed out a long sigh of relief.

8

—◆—

HUNTED

Kimberley awoke with a start, like something had touched her in the darkness of the empty carriage. Eyes wide, she scanned her surroundings and could only see the broken mirror and makeshift table.

'John?' She hushed and threw the blanket from her torso. 'John, are you there?'

Getting no answer, Kimberley swung her feet over the edge of the makeshift bed and scanned the platform outside of the carriage. To her surprise, the platform was no longer bathed in light. Heavy shadows now concealed much of the platform, and the only source of light came from a flaming barrel a little way along the platform from the carriage she occupied. Struggling to search for any sign of John, she was about to move when a solid arm wrapped around her neck and dragged her back. Before she could make a sound, she felt a gloved hand press over her mouth and, to her relief, heard John's voice whisper in her ear.

'Keep quiet. We're not alone.'

'Who?' Kimberley hissed as she pulled his hand from her mouth.

'Them.'

John pointed out of the window and at first Kimberley could see nothing on the platform beyond. Finally, something moved in the shadows and Kimberley watched as a pair of Imps trotted out into the light cast by the flaming barrel. Holding her breath, she watched as the pair shared a brief conversation and split to explore opposite ends of the station.

'What are we going to do? Are you going to fight them?'

'I think it's safer we hide, rather than fight.' John offered with a raised eyebrow.

'Wait, you're actually choosing not to show off your skills and prowess to impress me?'

'Sometimes it's helpful to stay hidden.'

'I never thought I'd hear you say that.' Kimberley joked as John released his grip on her.

'Follow me, and stay low.' John hushed as he dropped low and moved along the length of the carriage. 'I doubt there will only be two of them, and I doubt they'll be alone.'

'Revenants?' Kimberley pressed as she followed.

Offering only a nod in response, John reached the cracked mirror and slipped his hand between the back of the mirror and wall. Hearing a loud *crack*, Kimberley half expected the glass to come tumble down, alerting the searching Imps as to their presence. Instead, the mirror moved forward as John pulled it to the side. Exposing a small opening, Kimberley realised it was a service hatch leading down underneath the awkwardly positioned carriage.

'Ladies first.' John offered a coy smile and Kimberley felt the tension ease a little with his familiar joviality returning.

'Such the gentleman.' She was about to say more when an Imp jumped up onto the carriage roof.

'Quick.' John hushed and pressed his finger to his lips.

Pushing through the sea of cobwebs, Kimberley fought back the sudden fear of oversized spiders and insects crawling over her, and dropped through the small service hatch. Giving her eyes time to adjust to the darkness, she moved aside as John followed her in and pulled the mirror shut behind him. Plunged into darkness, Kimberley squeezed herself back, giving John enough room to take a seat beside her.

'What now?'

'We wait and hope they leave us be.'

'Won't they be able to know we are here?'

'Not the Imps, perhaps the Revenants but we're shrouded enough by me.'

'Sure about that?'

'No!' Despite the darkness, John shared an unseen playful smile. 'But you have to admit, it was better than me simply saying we're in trouble.'

Outside the carriage, the two Imps searched the length and breadth of the platform finding no sign of Kimberley or John. Frustrated by the lack of any sign of Kimberley or John, one Imp sent the barrel of flames clattering to the floor. Flaming logs spread in all directions as the creature released a cry of frustration that echoed around the old station.

'I sense something,' the lead Revenant declared as it stalked from a shadowy tunnel. 'But it feels distant.'

'Are they here?' Another Revenant quizzed as the remaining three joined it on the platform.

'It's hard to say.' The Revenant confessed as it sniffed the air. 'They've most certainly been here, but whether they remain, I doubt it.'

Sharing the Imp's frustration, the lead Revenant lifted a flaming log from the ground and admired the dancing flames as they encircled the log. Allowing its fingers to tease the dancing flames, the Revenant allowed its hand to set alight and showed no recognition of heat or pain as the flames crept along the length of its arm.

'Regardless of that,' the Revenant hissed as it looked to its companions. 'This place will no longer offer them safety or sanctuary.'

The flames that enveloped the Revenant's arm suddenly turned a blood-red colour, similar to the crystal heart left behind by the Ripper. Admiring the brightness of the flame, the accompanying Revenants stepped back, fearful of the flame, as the lead Revenant clenched its fist before slamming it down onto the tiled platform. The power of the blow cracked the tiled ground and in an instant the flames disappeared into the spiderweb of cracks, disappearing from view.

'You will burn this place?' One Imp gasped as the far wall exploded, sending sparks of crimson flame in all directions.

'Hell Fire will consume anything of our world.' The Revenant hissed as another section of wall erupted into flame. 'Anything he has left here will be destroyed.'

'We should move.' The Imp protested, fearful of a snaking flame that crept along the cracked platform towards it. 'This will kill us, too.'

'That it will.' Offering a twisted smile, the Imp was grateful to be dismissed and joined its companion in fleeing the burning station.

'And what of us?' Another of the Revenants quizzed. 'Hell Fire is lethal to us too'

'You're free to leave,' the Revenant hissed, its attention fixed on the flames that now consumed the entire far wall of the platform. 'I will remain, in the hope they return.'

'But...' the protest was silenced as the Revenant slammed a fist into its companion's face.

'You are free to leave.' The Revenant repeated. 'I will wait.'

'So be it.' Leaving it alone, the other three Revenants scampered away.

Alone on the platform, the Revenant traced the movement of the crimson flames and picked his position atop the listing carriage. Alone, surrounded by the crackling Hell Fire, his lifeless eyes scanned the vast platform, searching for any sign of movement. Careful to keep himself from the fire, the Revenant knew it was condemning itself to a painful end. It did so willingly, in the hope John would still be here. The taste of his adversary in the air was weak, distant, and hard to discern, but something about it told the Revenant John was not as far away as his senses told him.

Despite their hiding place, as the sound of flames grew, John knew they would have to move. Sensing the Hell Fire, John turned to Kimberley and pressed himself close so he could whisper in her ear.

'This won't be pleasant.'

'What?'

'See those flames?' John pointed through a small opening in the wall ahead of them where the crimson light had started to burn. 'They're Hell Fire, deadly to both of us.'

'Are they still out there?' There was panic in her voice.

'I'd be surprised if not, so we need to seize the element of surprise.'

'Am I going to die?' Kimberley's voice quivered.

'I'll do my best to make sure you don't.'

'That's encouraging.'

Ignoring Kimberley's reply, John called the plague doctor mask to his face and reached up to push the mirrored door open as quietly as he could.

'Stay close to me.' John hissed as he peeked through the opening. 'If you see a chance to escape, take it.'

'Where am I going to go?'

'Anywhere but here.' Looking down at her, plumes of smoke billowed in through the opening. 'Take this and use it if you need to.'

Reaching behind his back, John offered the Moon Blade for Kimberley to take. Pulling the neck of her top up over her mouth to save from choking on the smoke rolling in through the open mirror, Kimberley reluctantly took the curious weapon. Looking up at John, she was grateful the Raven's mask hid his face as she expected he would offer some feigned playful look to calm her nervousness.

'Won't you need it?' She quizzed as she admired the shimmering blade in the growing crimson light.

'Most likely, but I'm hardly useless without it.'

Pushing open the mirror, John clambered back into the smoke-filled carriage and turned to offer Kimberley his hand. Pulling her up, it dawned on him how quickly the Hell Fire had consumed the platform, as it filled the air with smoke and the crescendo of crackling flames. Peeking out of the windows, John saw the walls were ablaze and the platform itself offered a mishmash of paths through the roaring flames that gushed from the snaking cracks in the platform tiles.

'We're going to need to move.' John cursed. 'We haven't got much time.'

'Come little Raven.' The Revenant boomed as it dropped from the roof. 'I thought you were here, but I couldn't be sure.'

Seeing the dark figure drop to the platform, John saw the Revenant framed by the crimson flames as it turned to face the carriage. Knowing they were trapped, John turned to look at Kimberley.

'I'll meet you in Trafalgar Square.' John offered as he stalked to the door of the carriage. 'Trust nobody else.'

'What are you going to do?'

'Make sure you can escape.'

As ridiculous as it was, John offered Kimberley a thumbs up as he kicked the door open and burst out onto the platform. Fighting against the smoke filling the carriage, she could only watch as the two adversaries met on the flaming platform.

'Raven.' The Revenant snarled as it produced a crooked sword from its back.

'Lap dog!' John replied, his escrima sticks in hand. 'Just flames? Maybe we should add some of my smoke for decoration.'

Swirling orbs of smoke appeared around the flaming platform, the largest of which appeared in the air behind the Revenant's head. Seeing the creature's nervousness, John took that as a sign and attacked.

Diving over a tendril of crimson flame, John delivered two well-placed attacks on the Revenant's shoulder and head before it could even ready itself. Blocking the panicked attack with a solid kick, John clearly had the advantage as the two of them engaged in a furious fight that dragged them away from the carriage, giving Kimberley her chance to escape.

Keeping his focus on the Revenant, John did his best to keep the Revenant's attention with an onslaught of attacks and parries.

Despite her desire to help, unlike John and the Revenant, Kimberley knew the smoke slowly filling the station could kill her. As John dragged the revenant away from the carriage, seeing him deliver his attacks with surprising speed and accuracy, Kimberley made her move and burst out of the carriage. Immediately, her ears were filled with the terrifying screams and crackling of the blood-red flames that appeared like an impossible labyrinth between her and the only route she knew out of the subterranean station.

Moving as fast as she dared, Kimberley felt the heat from the flames that had almost consumed every inch of their hideaway. Keeping herself low, Kimberley shrieked as John and the Revenant crashed head over feet through the flames a little way ahead of her. Seeing the two supernatural creatures locked in battle, she realised how impossible this all was.

Coughing against the choking smoke, by the time she could see the narrow tunnel away from the platform, she had been forced onto her hands and knees by the smoke and flames. Scrambling across the battered platform, Kimberley was grateful to feel the cool air as she burst into the tunnel and ripped her top from her mouth and swallowed a lungful of air.

Feeling her body shake through fear and exertion, she was unaware of the Imp hidden in the shadows that followed her through the labyrinth of tunnels away from the station. Desperate to be free of the claustrophobic tunnels, she paid no attention to the path behind her, had she done so, she may have seen the skulking Imp following a way behind.

9

TARNISHED BLADE

Crashing through the roof of the station, the Revenant had gathered enough of an advantage to send the pair of them up and through the ceiling. Propelled with the force of the attack, John felt himself dragged through the concrete and metal until they exploded up into the next underground tunnel that ran above the station. Released from the Revenant's grasp, John smashed into the wall and slumped down, the crackle of electricity filling the air.

Shaking off the disorientation, John realised their collision had destroyed the now sparking track of the underground line. Electricity arced from the snapped lines, sending tendrils of electricity in all directions.

'Seeing you fight, I'm disappointed you could best the Ripper.' The Revenant snarled as it grasped the distorted metal and ripped it from the ground.

'Haven't we fought before?' John mocked as he rose to his feet, brushing off the dust and debris from his torso.

'I haven't had the pleasure, or disappointment as it would seem.' Using the snapped trainline, the Revenant slammed it into John, sending him crashing back into the wall.

'Really? You all look so familiar.'

The Revenant slammed the metal into him again before pinning John back against the grime-covered wall. Pushing the metal against John's throat, the Revenant could see its reflection in the scuffed lens of John's mask.

'You don't take your duty seriously.' The Revenant snarled as it slammed its head into the mask. 'Fight me.'

John knew he would have to put effort into their fight at some point. As they had danced around the burning station, he had done enough to keep the Revenant at bay and his attention away so Kimberley could escape. Giving the Revenant the advantage, he did little to fight back as the creature pressed the metal bar across his chest.

'You wouldn't want me to fight you.'

'That's exactly what I want!'

'So be it.'

Knowing he had given Kimberley enough time, John took hold of the metal and dragged it down and off his body. Before the Revenant could react, John pressed away from the wall and launched himself up and over the surprised creature. Turning the tables, John slammed the Revenant in the wall with great satisfaction. Wasting no time, John took hold of the Revenant's shoulder and tossed it further along the dark tunnel.

As the creature flew, John sprinted behind, launching himself to run along the wall and up onto the ceiling of the circular tunnel. Slamming into the wall, the Revenant had no time to react as John was upon him again and dropped from the ceiling.

'You wanted to see me and my powers?' John growled as he took hold of the Revenant's neck. 'Let me show you what you want to see of me.'

There was something different with John's voice. As he spoke, his words sounded rougher, hoarser, as he growled through the leather mask. With the Revenant dragging behind him, its legs flailing uncontrollably as it fought to break free, John sprinted along the length of the twisting underground tunnel until a light caught his attention in the distance.

Realising it was a train barreling towards them, John skidded to a halt on the tracks and pushed the Revenant down onto the ground.

'Fight me.'

'You're not worth my attention,' John replied as he watched the train careering towards them.

'Yes, I am.'

Before John could react, the Revenant prised itself free from John's grasp and used the power of darkness to send John crashing into the wall. Completely surprised by the attack, John felt the pain in his chest as the Revenant fought to wrap its unseen powers around him and hold him back. Fighting against the dark magic, John waited for the inevitable as the train drew nearer.

Knowing he would have one chance, John timed his attack with military precision. Shrugging free of the tightening grip of the Revenant's dark magic at the last second, John span and slammed the escrima stick into the side of the Revenant's head.

'This isn't their fight,' John warned as he enveloped himself and the Revenant in his shielding as the train reached them.

As the train moved at laboured speed, the concealment John had given them allowed the train to pass through them. Seeing the oblivious passengers whipping past, John felt a wave of relief that they remained unaware of him. Seeing the Revenant fighting against his control, John's heart sank as the Revenant offered him a hideously twisted grin and slammed its fist into the floor of the underground train.

Breaking free of John's spell, the metal floor buckled beneath the Revenant's fist and the train lurched on the tracks. As the scream of the emergency brakes filled the air, John took hold of the Revenant and launched them both up through the ceiling of the tunnel. Allowing the train to come to a stop beneath them, John drove them up through the levels until they crashed through the pavement and into the harsh daylight.

Ensuring they remained unseen, wrapping the Revenant once again in his spell, John's heart sank as he glimpsed Nelson's column between the buildings. Realising they were so close, John once again knew he needed to occupy the Revenant to ensure Kimberley would be free from its attention.

'You hide in the shadows to protect them,' the Revenant hissed as it dusted itself off. 'That's what makes it easier to defeat you. Hiding means you'll never be missed.'

'Care to tell me what you want with me?' John offered as he waited for their fight to resume.

'You'll know soon enough.'

John heard them before he saw them as the three other Revenant's dropped from the rooftops onto the street behind him. Surrounded, John looked at each of the Revenants and realised how obvious their differences were. Each creature looked different in some way, making him realise he had misjudged them as nothing more than dumb subservient creatures. Turning his attention back to the lead creature, John offered an almost respectful nod as he removed his coat and brushed back his hair from the front of the plague doctor mask.

'For no other reason than our own protection, we shall respect your shroud from the living.'

'Thanks.'

Seeing the flippant reply irritated the Revenants, it came as no surprise when they attacked in unison.

John did well to keep them all at bay. Unlike staged fights, this was not a fair display. Relentless in their attacks, all four moved at the same time to keep John from finding his rhythm to discard their attacks. Where he would fix his attention on one, another of the Revenants would deliver a blow to distract him enough to allow another. Feeling his body smashed back and forth, his senses soon started shutting down and stars danced in his vision.

Flailing blindly, the occasional attack would land but with nowhere near enough force to disturb the relentless attacks. Fighting for his survival, a searing pain traced down his back as a Revenant dragged its nails from his shoulder blade diagonally down to his hip. Knees buckling with the power, John raised his arm to cover his head as it threw a solid kick towards his face.

Blind luck allowed him to block the attack, and in a split second, he took hold of the solid leg and pulled with all his strength. Fed by the Revenant's momentum, John dropped back and hurled the Revenant over his head. Sending the creature flying through the air, he felt a brief satisfaction as the creature slammed into a lamppost, snapping it in two to come crashing down on a parked car.

Whatever people there were, could still not see the fighting creatures camouflaged from their consciousness. The air was filled with the blaring horn from the damaged car, but nobody paid it any mind. Distracted by the sound, John panicked as a hand wrapped around his neck and dragged him up through the air. Feeling his legs lift from the floor, John realised it was the lead Revenant who had him in its grasp and panicked as he felt himself slammed into the wall of the National Gallery loading bay.

Feeling the roller shutters strain against the increased pressure, John desperately fought to find purchase but all the shutters could do was sag back, giving him no way to push back against the Revenant. Joined by one other, John could only watch as fist after fist was slammed against the side of his head.

At last, the lead Revenant ripped the plague doctor mask from his face and smiled at the look of deflated defeated on John's battered face.

'Had enough?' the Revenant hissed as it pressed its face to John's. 'I can taste your fear.'

As grotesque as it was, the Revenant *licked* the length of John's face, sending an uncontrollable shudder of disgust through him.

'Kill him.' The accompanying Revenant jibed with excitement.

'I can still taste the humanity in you, like a virus that continues to hold you.'

'At least I have a past.' John choked against the brutal grip at his throat. 'You're nothing but an empty, lifeless thing from the shadows.'

'That may be,' the Revenant spat. 'But your protection of these things makes you weak. You cannot ever embrace your true power until you stop hiding.'

Slamming its solid fist into his face, John's head smashed against the metal. Knowing he was overpowered and out skilled, John's mind raced for a way to escape, but the words from the third Revenant destroyed any sense of a plan forming in his head.

'She's here.' The creature that had been slammed into the lamppost declared as it turned its nose towards the sky. 'His bitch, she's near.'

'You've got me, that's enough.' John's heart sank, knowing they were a stone's throw away from Trafalgar Square and where he had agreed to meet Kimberley.

'That care you carry for them, it really is your greatest weakness.' The lead Revenant mocked as it dismissed the other to hunt Kimberley down. 'While ever you protect them, you'll never beat us.'

Seeing the Revenant disappear, John's frustration increased. Acting out of pure desperation and, although he hated to admit it, fear for Kimberley, he allowed his weight to sag and pulled the Revenant closer. In doing so, the creature was pulled off-balance, giving him a split second of purchase on the concrete path. Taking full advantage, John pushed himself up and drove his elbow up underneath the creature's chin with enough force to break free of its vice-like grip.

'I'm their protector,' John screamed as he delivered a second and third elbow to the Revenant's head. 'What good would I be if I abandoned them.'

Another of the creatures launched through the air and landed on his back, dragging him away from the furiously dazed leader. Moving with the momentum of the surprise attack, John slammed the Revenant on his back against the wall and felt its grip loosen enough to pull himself free.

What happened next caught John by surprise. It was the strange feeling of numbness that told him something was wrong. Having sensed a movement, he had expected to feel another attack, but he felt nothing, absolutely nothing. Looking down at his chest, John's mind raced as he saw the handle of a crooked dagger protruding from the right side of his stomach. The immediate area around the blade felt completely numb. As he staggered back and reached for the handle, his fingers felt alight the moment his fingertips touched the weapon.

'What is this?' John coughed, the movement of air in his lungs feeling like a raging fire burned inside him.

'That is a tarnished blade, a gift from me, to you.' The crooked grin on the disfigured face told John all he needed to know.

Once again, he reached for the protruding handle but pulled away as the pain erupted through his hand. Fearing what the blade was doing, John was desperate to escape, and his mind raced in a million directions. Barreling through the mocking Revenant, he heard the lead creature's mocking laughter as he launched along the side street and staggered towards Trafalgar Square.

'Let him go for his pet. It may do him well to see her die.'

Ignoring the echoing voice, John staggered down the street. Although he felt the searing pain with each breath, he also felt the numbness spreading from the wound in his stomach. John knew whatever dark magic had tarnished the blade was doing something terrible to his body and he needed to be rid of it. That said, he also knew Kimberley would walk into a trap and he was the only one who could protect her.

Bursting into Trafalgar Square, the sky was bathed in the eerie glow of sunset, and he scanned the meandering crowds for any sign of Kimberley. Seeing the Revenant poised beside the impressive statue of Nelson, John lowered his gaze and spotted Kimberley moving through the crowds to the base of the infamous column. Moving as fast as he could, John staggered down the steps in front of the National Gallery and called her name as the Revenant dropped from its perch.

'Kimberley, NO!.'

10

INTO THE LIGHT

Kimberley's eyes went wide as she saw John staggering down the steps and the Revenant drop to the ground between them. Seeing the creature unfold itself, Kimberley backed away, but John knew he was in no position to fight. Hearing the hurried footfalls behind him, he knew the other Revenants were racing to join them. Mind racing despite the pulsating pain and spreading numbness, John knew they were trapped.

'Finish her and be done with it.' The lead revenant boomed as it stood at the top of the steps looking down at them.

'Leave her alone.' John choked.

"Too much care, you'll be better if we sever your connection to their pathetic lives.'

Turning his back on the lead, John's attention fixed on the lone Revenant as he limped across the square towards it. Fixing his gaze on the muscular creature, he ignored Kimberley's terrified expression as she looked around at the ignorant crowds of meandering people. The square was filled with people of every type. Business people marched through the crowds of tourists and families as they took in the spectacular historical landmark, and yet they all saw nothing of the interaction playing our in front of them.

Feeling his knees buckle beneath him, John made it halfway to Kimberley as the Revenant extended its claws and offered him a victorious smile. Knowing he could do nothing to protect her, John's desperation offered him the only impossible solution. Scanning the rooftops for any sign of Azrael, John knew he had to make his own decision. Closing his eyes, taking a moment to compose himself, it was Kimberley's yelp of fear that dragged him back and decided for him.

Pushing his fists into the concrete, John fought against the pain to rise from the ground. Locking his gaze on the Revenant, John clenched his fists tight and offered his desperate last act to protect Kimberley.

'She's not yours to take.' John hollered as he pushed through the pain and closed the Revenant down. 'Leave her alone, or pay the price.'

'What price? You're broken, the tarnished blade is draining your powers.' The Revenant did not even turn to look at John, dismissing his warning with utter contempt.

'Last chance, lap dog.'

'Or else what?'

Having moved close enough to the Revenant and Kimberley, John opened his hands and muttered something in a language long unheard by human ears. Hearing the words, the Revenant froze in position and snatched its head around to look at him.

'What are you doing?' The panic was clear on its face.

'The one thing your foolish leader reminded me about.'

Finishing the ancient ritual, John waited. Had he been able to breathe, he would have held his breath, but instead he simply waited for the inevitable change. Frozen in place, the Revenant cast a glance towards its three companions, who were hastily retreating away from the staircase down into the square.

'Fool.'

'That may be. But it is done.' With a clock of his fingers, the world froze for a second around them. Only Kimberley, John and the Revenants could move as everyone else around them was rooted where they were.

'What's happening?' Kimberley gasped as she saw a young child mid-run chasing a pigeon that was suspended in the air, wings spread but unmoving in the air.

'I'm lifting the shroud.'

As the three Revenants made good their escape, the fourth turned and sprinted in hot pursuit. As it launched past John, he turned and offered the panicked creature one final remark.

'Bit late for that.'

It happened like a shockwave, John being its epicentre as it filled the air with an enormous rumble of thunder. From the clear dusk sky, a single bolt of lightning crashed to down, colliding with John and enveloping him in a column of burning bright light. Shielding her eyes, Kimberley did not see what happened next. The fleeing Revenant felt the solid impact as the shockwave crashed into its back and sent it slamming into the bottom of the stone steps.

When the lightning ended, John remained standing in the same spot, the tarnished blade no longer embedded in his stomach, but lying at his feet on the charred ground. Turning to look for the Revenant, John smiled at the look of sheer panic on the creatures face as he stalked towards it.

'What have you done?' The Revenant stammered as it backed away from him.

Before he could answer, Trafalgar Square was filled with panicked screams as John and the Revenant were no longer hidden from view by the shroud of dark magic that had kept them camouflaged. Quickly calling the plague doctor mask to his face, John surged forward and attacked the fleeing creature. Still feeling the pulsating pain in his stomach, it was no longer debilitating and he could ignore the pain as he returned to his persona as the Raven.

Panic set in amongst the gathered crowds in Trafalgar Square. Those of the afterlife who had been touched by the shockwave that emanated from John were no longer hidden. Expecting the other three Revenants had made good their escape, John could only smile as another wave of panic surged from the front of the National Gallery above them.

'Looks like your friends didn't quite make it.'

'Neither did you.' The Revenant spat as she scrambled up the stairs away from him.

'That was my sacrifice to make.' John reached for the escrima sticks but stopped at the sound of Kimberley's voice.

'Wait!' She hollered over the panicked crowds, grabbing their belonging and loved ones to flee the grotesque sight of the Revenant. 'You'll need this.'

Smiling beneath the mask, John watched as Kimberley threw the Moon Blade across to him. Watching it arc through the air, John casually caught the blade by the handle as the Revenant made it halfway up the wide steps. Feeling all eyes on him, John took full advantage of his position centre stage and made his grand reveal to the masses a spectacular display of strength and power.

Launching himself into the air, his coat billowing behind him, John somersaulted through the air to land at the top of the steps ahead of the Revenant. Holding his head to one side, giving his expressionless mask a somewhat quizzical look, John spoke so only the Revenant could hear him. Catching sight of the sea of camera phones now pointed at him, John knew he had to show the world his true nature and identity as the Raven.

'What say we give them a show?'

'You're mad!'

'It's been said before,' John mocked as he tested the weight of the Moon Blade in his hand. 'But I think you'll find I'm just dangerous.'

Expecting the attack, the Revenant ripped the dagger from its leg as John drove the Moon Blade down towards its head. Having the higher ground made it easier to force the Revenant back down the steps. Dodging from side-to-side, John felt invigorated and alive. Calling every ounce of his strength back to him, he made quick work of forcing the Revenant back down to the open square.

Reaching the flatter ground, the Revenant fought back but found each attack thwarted by John. Awash with desperation, their fight continued back towards the impressive base of Nelson's column.

'End it now.' The Revenant hissed as the Moon Blade slashed across its chest, leaving a smouldering gash in its wake. 'We both know you've won.'

'And deny them their show? I don't think so.' John feigned an attack with the blade but slammed a fist into the Revenant's face, sending it crashing into the stone base.

'This isn't a game.'

'It's very much a game.' John corrected as he drove forward and pressed the curved blade against the Revenant's throat. 'By bringing me into the light, you and your bastard friends will have a harder time taking me in.'

'All you're doing is delaying the inevitable and risking more of these pathetic beings you swear to protect.'

'You'll be forced to act with more caution if they know we exist.'

'They'll send more of us to find you.'

'And I'll be waiting for them.'

'We both will.' Kimberley added as she moved to join John at the base of the iconic landmark. 'We should go. Everyone's watching.'

'I'm counting on it.' John hissed as he released his grasp on the Revenant and stepped back.

'You're letting me go?'

'No, I'm just letting them get a better view.'

Before the Revenant could react, John rotated on the spot and punched the Moon Blade straight forward. Passing through its neck with ease, the Revenant's eyes went wide as the blade buried into the polished stone and severed the head in a single blow. Balancing on his hand, the creature's body dropped like a stone at his feet.

'Was that necessary?' Kimberley barked as she saw the sea of eyes watching them, amongst them the terrified faces of children mixed among them. 'There are kids.'

'The world needs to see this, it needs to see what's happening.' John replied as he pulled his hand back and allowed the head to tumble to the ground. 'It's the only way we're going to survive this.'

Whispering something under his breath, the crowd gasped and Kimberley yelped as the decapitated body burst into flames and disintegrated into a pile of dust in a matter of seconds. Hearing the nervous chatter among the gathered crowds, John knew he had their attention. Pushing past Kimberley, he moved her behind him to shield her as much as he could.

'What are you?' A nervous voice blurted from the crowd.

'I am the Raven.' John declared, swelling with feigned pride. 'Remember this face, and pray that when these things hunt you, it's me you see and not them.'

'What do you mean?'

'I am your protector from the creatures that would haunt your nightmares.'

Taking Kimberley's hand, he launched them through the square at an impossible speed. Leaving no trace of them behind, he felt Kimberley's hands dig into his arm as he lifted them up into the air and found his familiar rooftop overlooking the square. Knowing the rapid movement would send her body into turmoil, John opted for the nearest rooftop and placed her down gently.

'Take a moment, don't panic.' John soothed as he ripped the plague doctor mask from his face.

'I can't breathe.' Kimberley stammered as she felt her lungs refusing to respond to her demand for air.

'It'll pass, give it a moment.'

At last the air rushed down her throat and the blue tinge to her skin immediately disappeared. Leaving her resting against the weathered gargoyle, John moved to the raised edge of the rooftop and looked down at the dumbstruck crowds they had left behind. Seeing their confusion, John felt a heavy weight at what he had sacrificed. Although he had always existed in plain site with his human appearance, his guise as the Raven had always been hidden from the masses, providing him the means to blend in and protect them. Slumping forward, he released a long sigh as he allowed the gravity to sink in.

'Why did you do that?' Kimberley pressed as she gingerly rose to join him on the roof's edge. 'Isn't it dangerous?'

'It was necessary,' John sighed. 'They were more determined than I've ever experienced. Whatever purpose drove them, meant they will risk everything to take me to their masters.'

'Risk things how?'

'Manifesting Hell Fire in the living realm, brandishing a tarnished blade. Those are forbidden things, they risk upsetting the balance and bringing the might of Azrael to sever their connection to this world indefinitely.'

'But why would they do that?'

'I still haven't worked that out, which scares me even more.'

'But by giving up your ability to hide, won't that unbalance everything?'

'It'll give me the ability to be seen. If I'm seen, it makes it harder for the Revenants to attack me.'

'You mean us? There's no denying I'm stuck with you now.'

'I'm sorry about that, I really am.'

John watched as a trio of police cars arrived at the square, blue lights reflecting in all directions as darkness descended.

'I think we are past apologies. Why don't we finally work out what is going on and put a stop to it?'

'I think things are about to get a lot messier for us.'

'You've just decapitated a monster in the middle of London. What can be messier than that.'

'Do you know what scares me the most? I just don't know, but I expect we've not seen the last of the other Revenants and the Full Moon Society.'

Watching from the shadow of the gargoyle, the pair could only speculate what awaited them on the treacherous path they we. Sharing no more words, they watched as Trafalgar Square became a hive of police activity.

The Raven was no longer a forgotten sentinel; he was now, most certainly to be remembered.

—•—

EPISODE

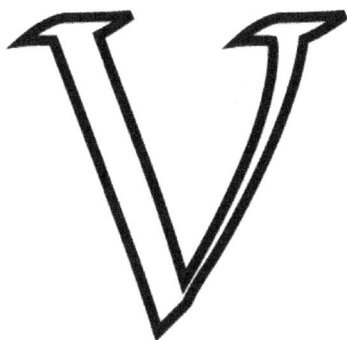

SACRIFICE

11

IN THE SHADOWS

Almost a week had passed and neither John nor Kimberley had seen any sign of the Revenants. Scouring the internet for news, there had been a frenzy of media attention around John's dramatic reveal in Trafalgar Square, but pretty soon it had become old news. Suspecting there were forces at play to suppress the dramatic revelation, it had soon fallen too quiet for either of their liking.

'You can always tell the interfering fingers of power.' John scoffed as he tossed the tablet to Kimberley. 'I'm now described as a poor attempt at a magic act.'

'The Society?' Kimberley mused as she skimmed through the article.

'Who else?' John's frustration was palpable as he dropped into the seat.

'Well, they're playing you at your own game,' Kimberley replied as she showed John his maskless face. 'Seems they've gone loud with your escape from the Nuthall, though they obviously haven't linked your theatrics in Trafalgar Square.'

'Maybe we should connect the dots for them.'

'I think the public have seen enough for now.' Kimberley knew their confinement in the cheap hotel was feeding John's frustration, but it had to be done.

It had been easier for Kimberley to change her appearance enough to blend in with the crowds of London. Not wanting to flee the capital, knowing the ties of the Society to the city, meant they would have to survive as best they could, given the circumstances. Having cut her hair and dyed it black, with the right amount of make-up and clothes to obscure her face, she could easily blend in and disappear among the crowds. Despite his best efforts, John's face was all over London and he knew the curious gazes would recognise him in an instant.

'What do you suppose we do? This is like being back in the Nuthall, except I can feel everything.'

'What do you mean?'

'Hand!' John barked and held out his hand for her to take.

Knowing better than to question, Kimberley offered an exacerbated sigh and moved to join him. Pressing her hand to his, she felt the familiar swirling in her stomach, but this time the world around her did not collapse. Whereas before she had found herself transported into the past, this was something entirely different. The world around her stayed the same, except it now had a peculiar amber hue. Taking a moment to compose herself, Kimberley turned to look at John, who once again had his lopsided smile and swagger of confidence.

'Care to take a walk?' John offered as he moved to the hotel room door.

'You shouldn't leave.' She protested as he gripped the handle.

'Don't panic yourself, we're still sitting in the room like we are when we talk a trip down memory lane. This is us exploring the world from my perspective.'

Opening the door, John stepped aside, allowing Kimberley a view into the corridor. Gasping, it took a few seconds to register what she was seeing. Just beyond the door, she could see pulsating lines like veins of all different colours, stretching in either direction. The sheer volume covered the walls and ceiling, leaving only the floor clear of the strange pulsating veins.

'What are they?'

'It's hard to explain, but think of them as memory lines. They're very temporary in their existence and quick to fade. Sometimes I can enter them, and other times they are nothing more than whispers of events.'

'Why are you showing them to me?'

'Because you'll see what I see, then maybe you can feel how isolating this gift is.'

Taking her hand, John scanned the plethora of veins and chose one. Moving her arm, he felt her reluctance, but pressed her hand against one vein and watched her reaction. Seeing her tense, John hung on her movements and waited to see her expression change. Doing his best to stay calm, he saw her eyes flicker left and right behind her eyelids as she struggled to find her way around the cascading waterfall of memories and visions he knew would now swim through her mind.

'Breathe,' John soothed as he saw her body tense. 'Don't fight it. Let the flow and take you wherever it needs to.'

Whispering in her ear, John longed to take hold of her but knew better of it. With her navigating the lines, any intervention from him would sever her connection and break her concentration. Fighting his own impatience, he jumped back as she recoiled away from the veins and opened her eyes.

'They're here!' Kimberley gasped as she gasped for breath. 'They're coming to find us.'

'Revenants?' John pressed as he caught her mid-fall.

'No, but people who have been touched by them. I could sense them, but not see them.' John lowered her to the ground as the amber-hue world was replaced with the familiar hotel room. 'They're human!'

'That's debatable.' John scoffed as he reached for the plague doctor mask on the table beside the window.

'Who are they?'

'They will be members of the Society.' John declared as he moved to the door.

'Wait, where are you going?'

'To stop them, obviously.'

'You can't.' Kimberley fought to stand up but her legs refused to move. 'They'll know we're here.'

'I think they might know already.' John chuckled as he stood over her. 'Where were they?'

'You knew, didn't you?' Once again, Kimberley realised John had played her. 'That's why you made me touch it, isn't it?'

'You're learning.' John offered her a playful smile that did nothing to melt the frustration she felt.

'We are in this together you know.' Kimberley's boomed. 'You're going to have to trust me at some point.'

'I do trust you. I would have thought that was clear by now.' Sliding the mask over his face, John pulled the hood over his head as he spoke. 'If you'd gone looking for them with knowledge why you were there, they would have known.'

'They're not Revenants.' Kimberley protested.

'No, but like you said, they've been touched by them. They'll feed them and any sign you were looking. I protected you by not telling you.'

'Being with you is like being on the worst rollercoaster in the world. I never know which way I'm facing or what's coming next.'

'Stay in the room, leave this to me.' Making no apology, John yanked the door opened and disappeared from view.

As the door closed behind him, John couldn't shake the feeling of guilt he had towards Kimberley. He knew his games were taking their toll on her, and she deserved better. All the young woman had been through in the weeks since meeting him in the dark interview room in the Nuthall, the least he could do was show her the trust he had in her. Comforting himself in the fact his deceptions were a necessary evil, John shrugged off the distraction of his thoughts and made his way through the interior of the hotel.

Daring to connect with his supernatural senses, John saw enough in the shadows of the afterlife to direct him towards the roof of the dingy hotel. The walls were stained and in need of a coat of fresh paint. In fact, everything about the dark interior required attention. Reaching the staircase, John pushed open the door and sighed as the heavy door moved aside and then dropped from the hinges to rest against the wall.

'Even the Nuthall was better than this!'

Looking up through the centre of the staircase, John caught sight of a black sleeve and knew he had to proceed with caution. Changing his mind about using the stairs, John returned into the hallway and approached the nearest hotel room door. Making sure he was alone, John stepped up to the battered wooden door and simply walked *through* the secured wooden door. Once on the other side, his entry was welcomed with a shrill scream from the half-naked young woman who had just stepped out of the bathroom opposite.

Knowing a sudden scream in a salubrious establishment such as this would go ignored, he needed to ensure there were no more. Closing the distance between them in two strides, John clamped his hand over the woman's mouth and rotated her, bringing her to rest against his chest. Fighting against his grasp, John wrapped an arm across her neck and tightened until the strength left her fight. Slumping in his arms, he was careful to lay her on the stained sheets and cover her over to protect her modesty. Stepping back from the bed, John froze as the world flickered for a moment, taking him back to the murder scene of Mary Ann Nichols. The unconscious woman of the bed was laid in the exact same position as Mary's corpse and the sudden flashback sent him reeling for a moment.

Fighting to swim back from the vivid memory, John's senses returned when the fire alarm within the building sounded. Snatched back in an instant, he knew it was time to act and made his way outside without hesitation. Scaling the side of the building, John scrambled up over the gantry and made his way to the top of the staircase leading onto the roof. Surprised to find the fire escape door wedged open, John scanned the rooftop for any sign of a Revenant or guard poised with a view of the building's entrance.

Seeing nothing, he moved through the open door and immediately heard the voices a few levels below.

'Spotters have the doors. If they step out into the street, our sniper will take her out.'

'Not much they can do against him!' Another muffled voice replied.

'The Revenant is waiting. All we need to do is get the bracelets on him.'

Hearing mention of the dampening bracelets, John unconsciously rubbed his wrists as he formulated a plan of what to do.

'What if they don't come out?'

'Then we either clear this hell hole room by room, or we burn it to the ground.'

John had heard enough. Listening to the blatant disregard for the other inhabitants of the decrepit hotel reinforced his knowledge of the callous nature of the Full Moon Society. Feeling his anger rising, John pulled the Moon Blade from his back and looked down the gap in the centre of the staircase. Unable to see all of them, John counted at least seven men held on the concrete stairs. Clad in black combats and fatigues, each of them sported a modified respirator that left them looking like some curious apocalyptic mercenary on the dark staircase. Seeing only a few of them armed with guns, the rest of them carried weapons that John did not recognise.

Acutely aware of the Society's knowledge of the afterlife, having weapons he did not recognise added an air of caution to his next move. Weighing up all his options, John chose and moved to the edge of the banister. Climbing up onto the wooden handrail, he looked back towards the open door and admired the rooftop view of London stretching off into the distance.

Content with his choice, John turned his attention back down to his prey below and announced his presence.

'Gentlemen!' His muffled voice echoed in the stairwell.

As all eyes snapped around to look up towards his voice, none of them saw the smile on his face beneath the mask. Knowing he had their attention, John stepped off the bannister and dropped down the narrow gap in the middle of the staircase. Still with the Moon Blade in hand, John found his first mark as the blade cleanly cut through the forearm of the nearest attacker. Grabbing hold of the metal struts, John stopped his descent and propelled himself in among the gathered group.

'You should have chosen a different plan!' John hissed, his voice almost drowned out by the frenzied screams of pain from the injured man. 'But, you're here now. So let's dance.'

12

DEFIANCE

The stairwell was not the best place for a fight, but there was room enough for John to confrontation. Using the walls to launch himself up, over, around and through the squad of mercenaries. He despatched the first pair in a handful of moves, but the third was able to deflect John's attack as he sliced the Moon Blade through the air. Sensing the mercenary's intention, John caught sight of the dampening bracelet out of the corner of his eye.

Intercepting the subtle movement, John sliced the curved blade down the man's forearm. John felt satisfaction at the resistance as the blade tugged against fabric and flesh, accompanied by a shriek of pain. Retracting his hand, John saw the bracelet drop to the ground and wasted no time kicking it over the edge of the landing, sending it tumbling to the lower parts of the building.

Glad to be rid of the immediate threat, one mercenary took full advantage of the distraction and slammed the curious weapon into John's chest. The moment the hammerhead weapon collided with him, John felt a pain he had not felt in over a hundred years. Whatever dark magic had enchanted the weapon, they intended it to inflict pain on those existing in the world between life and death. Much like a feeling of fire beneath his flesh where he had been struck, John gasped as he staggered back and felt a pair of arms wrap around his upper body.

'Get the other one.' A muffled voice yelled from the respirator behind his head. 'I can't hold him long!'

Hearing the effort in the voice, John fought to break free of the vice-like grip. Feeling the arms weaken just a little, a fresh wave of burning pain exploded in his head as another of the weapons slammed into the side of his face. Unable to control his screaming senses, the world span as another figure moved with haste, the second dampening bracelet gripped tight in their hand.

'John!'

Her voice was enough to distract the would-be attacker and gave him enough time to rip free from the mercenary's grasp. Stumbling forward, John looked down to see Kimberley's face two levels below them, her eyes wide and face filled with terror.

'Run!' Was all he could muster before the attacks started again.

Their fight was more desperate, each attack delivered with venom and frustration, with John only just able to keep himself composed against each blow. Catching one attack, John bent the man's wrist until he felt the bone snap. Tearing the hammerhead weapon free, John smashed it into the man's temple and watched with satisfaction as unconsciousness swallowed him.

Armed now with a weapon in each hand, the remaining mercenaries were not prepared for the ferocious attacks John unleashed. Pushing aside the remnants of fog that swam in his head, John's connection with his powers were limited but enough to give him the advantage. Moving with impossible speed, John opted for a different tact and ripped the gloves from his hands as he rendered the first pair of masked men unconscious. Settling on the third, the one who now nursed the oozing wound on his forearm, John ripped the respirator free of his face and pressed his hand against his cheek.

The stairwell collapsed around them, and John manifested the pair of them atop the infamous clock-tower of Big Ben. Choosing to place them in his Victorian memories, John gave the startled man a moment to compose himself as they balanced precariously on a narrow ledge between the ornate decoration and the high-pitched roof. Shrouded by night, it satisfied John they would remain unnoticed by his memories meandering the London streets far below.

'Who are you?' John hissed from beneath the mask as the injured man scanned his surroundings wide-eyed. 'I won't ask again.'

'Where am I?' The young mercenary stammered as he nursed the jagged wound on his lower arm.

'Look at me.' John snarled as he pressed the hooked nose of the plague doctor mask to the man's face. 'You're not here to enjoy the sights, you're here to answer my questions.'

'Or else what?' The man had found enough composure to argue back with feigned confidence. 'I know this isn't real.'

'Oh, it's real enough.' John warned as he hoisted the man up and over the ledge in one surprising move. 'This may be nothing more than my memories, but if I leave you here, then you'll fit right in at the Nuthall Hospital.'

'Don't let me go.' The man screeched as he fought to hold on to John's arm. 'I'll tell you what you want.'

'Who sent you?'

'The Full Moon.'

'The warden?'

'They're all in this.' The man blurted, his words all but spewing out his mouth with the panic. 'They just want you.'

'And your part in this?' John snarled as he held the man out further.

'What do you mean?'

'Your part in this. Why are you here?'

'They sent us to bring you to them.'

'Why?'

'You'll find out.' A crooked smile appeared on the man's face as he stopped struggling and released his desperate grasp on John's arm.

'I'll drop you.'

'Do what you want. I've done my part.'

'Your part?'

'Distraction.'

The world disintegrated as the buildings collapsed as if they had been made from ash. As the view of Victorian London was replaced once again with the stairwell, John felt a familiar feeling consume his body as he stepped back and allowed the mercenary to drop to the ground, convulsing at his feet. Through the blue-hued lenses, John felt a wave of panic as he realised the distraction from the mercenary had been enough to allow the other bracelet to be snapped around his wrist.

Feeling his connection with the afterlife weakened, his mind raced to find a way to break free. Resorting to brute force, John slammed the head of the nearest mercenary into the metal bannister and tossed him over, allowing him to drop between the staircases down to the concrete below. Refusing to allow them any more of an advantage, John followed the body over the rail and dropped to the level where Kimberley had been.

Knowing their advantage would be short-lived, John sprinted along the corridor and crashed through the wooden door.

'Kimberley?' John yelled as he scanned the hotel room. 'Where are you?'

His movements felt laboured, as if he was moving through tar. Struggling to keep everything in focus, John staggered through the hotel room with no sign of Kimberley anywhere to be seen. Clearing the last room, John looked towards the open window and lurched forward as he saw the curtains moving in the breeze. Bursting onto the small balcony, John expected to find her cowering behind the wall, but found it empty.

Looking both ways, John heard the sound of a round being fired before he felt himself thrown into the brick wall by the sudden impact of the high-velocity round. Unable to the feel the pain from the bullet that had torn through his chest, John slid down the wall as a second round exploded in the brickwork where he had been. Showered by debris and dust, John knew he would be in the crosshairs of the sniper and although the rounds could do little to cause him harm, he did not need the distraction.

Crawling back into the hotel room, he dusted himself off and rose to his feet. Seeing his reflecting in the mirror, John saw how battered and broken he looked. His mask bore the scuffs of his fight on the stairwell and his chest was exposed through the tattered fabric where the round had passed through him. Seeing the bracelet in the reflection, John cursed as he admired the familiar silver that wrapped around his arm and was about to speak when a new sound stole his attention.

Even without turning, John knew what had landed on the balcony behind him. Feeling a cold chill on his back, there was no way he could muster the familiar flippant remarks as he turned to face the lead Revenant. Knowing his connection to his powers was limited, John knew he should run, but without knowing where Kimberley was, he could not risk leaving her to the Revenant or mercenaries in the stairwell.

'You don't seem yourself.' The Revenant oozed as it saun-tered into the dreary hotel room. 'I suppose this is a little better than the derelict ruins you prefer.'

'Where is she?' John growled as he fixed his attention on the Revenant.

'She won't be too far. I don't think we have her yet.'

'I take it this was your idea?' John feigned confidence as he wafted the dampening bracelet in front of him. 'The only way you can actually get an advantage over me.'

Stepping forward, the Revenant stopped itself as it realised John's goading had almost worked. Offering a sinister smile, John was about to reply when he sensed something behind him and moved without thought, slicing the Moon Blade through the air. Finding its mark, the curved blade killed the mercenary as it sliced through the man's chest and heart. Dropping to his knees, the body landed in an awkward position between John and the door.

'At least you'll still offer something of a challenge.' The Revenant drawled as John returned his attention to it. 'I'd hate to think I was fighting, just a man.'

'You should be so lucky. At least then, you may have stood a chance.'

The Revenant attacked, and despite his demands, John could not match the demon's speed. Feeling the first blow, he tried to dodge the second. Instead of another solid fist, the Revenant took hold of John's collar and launched him through the air and out of the open door into the corridor. Crashing into the wall,

John skidded on the well-trodden carpet and knew he was at a serious disadvantage being half-dampened.

Seeing the sleek frame of the Revenant stalk through the doorway John made his choice and ran. Turning his back on the creature, he sprinted along the long corridor and hurled himself around the corner as the lift door opened in front of him. Giving no warning to the terrified occupants of the battered lift, John hurled himself through the doors and promptly smashed his hand onto the button to close the door.

Hearing the young woman yelp in horror, John saw the Revenant round the corner as the door slid shut.

'You're that guy from the news!' The young man declared as he comforted the terrified woman.

'You should get off on the next floor. You don't want that thing thinking you helped me.' John replied as he ripped open the emergency hatch in the ceiling and leapt through it.

Climbing the cables, it pleased John the see the lift stopped on the next level. Knowing the Revenant, or whoever was waiting for him, would find nothing more than an empty lift, John scrambled back to the roof and made his escape from the tatty hotel. Hoping Kimberley had made her escape, John melted into the crowds of Londoners and made his way to their agreed meeting place, The Ten Bells pub.

13

THE TEN BELLS

G rateful for the anonymity of the masked crowds, John walked along Commercial Street and towards the public house. The exterior, while modernised, still resembled what he remembered from his time patrolling the streets before his death. More than once, John had found time to sneak a pint from the pub before returning home after a shift. Despite being one of the lesser frequented pubs by the constabulary, he had always found it a simple place to hide in plain sight. Now, amid modern London, the pub seemed a perfect fusion of the modern and historic elements of the capital.

'John?' Kimberley's voice carried over the chatter of the crowds.

Looking around, he couldn't help but grin beneath the mask as Kimberley was being dismissed by a burly man dressed in a similar style plague doctor mask. Seeing the sea of curious masks of all shapes and styles, for the first time, it was Kimberley who looked out of place.

'Sorry love, wrong guy.' The burly man replied but soon changed his tone as he took in Kimberley's appearance. 'That said sweety, I'd happily buy you a drink if you're up for it.'

'I'm alright, thanks.'

'She's with me.' John declared as he scooped Kimberley under the arm and guided her away from the man.

'Lucky sod.' Was all he heard as they moved deeper into the anonymity offered by the pub.

Moving through the door, John snatched a discarded crumpled leaflet from an empty table and moved through the busy pub. Guided by Kimberley, they made to the back of the pub and found a small table that would allow them to blend into the crowds. Swallowed by the chatter, the sound of voices and conversations was drowned out as John unfolded the leaflet and laid it on the table between them.

'What's with that?' Kimberley quizzed as she read the printed sheet.

'It's the reason they're all dressed as they are.' John answered as he scanned the busy room. 'It's certainly an advantage for me. Although you might want to get something to fit in.'

'What's a Blood Moon Festival?'

'Lunar eclipse.' A young woman interrupted as she scooped the empty glasses from the table. 'Some corporate sponsored event the brewery got involved with. Just an excuse for a piss-up, really.'

'Is it just in the pubs?' John pressed as the woman cleared the table.

'Find out for yourself.' She replied, tapping the leaflet. 'And if you're not buying a drink, would you mind moving on?'

As the clearly frustrated woman moved to the next table, both their attention returned to the crumpled leaflet. Whoever had arranged the festivities, had arranged for a street festival, carnival atmosphere and stalls for the length of Curtain Street in Shoreditch.

'Hardly the place for a lunar celebration.' John mused as he looked at the sheet. 'I doubt Shoreditch is any better than I remember it being.'

'It's actually quite alive nowadays.' Kimberley corrected as she scanned the crowds inside the pub. 'Doesn't seem an odd choice to me.'

'We see the worlds differently.' John mused.

'What do you see then?' Kimberley's frustration bubbled as she pushed the leaflet away. 'I don't have the luxury of your godly perspective.'

'What's wrong?'

'I'm tired.' Kimberley sighed and threw her head back to look up at the ceiling. 'I don't know how I made it out of that hotel. I just feel the whole world is watching my every move.'

'I need to end this, I know.' The roar of a boisterous group forced him to look around. 'It's not easy, but I know this isn't where you belong. I just need to overcome this little problem.'

Laying his hand on the table, John lifted his sleeve to show Kimberley the dampening bracelet on his wrist. Seeing the familiar bracelet, she snatched his arm and looked at it.

'How do I get it off?'

'Things are different now.' John offered a long sigh. 'The last time, we were unconnected and you had never interfered with the dark magic that makes them work. Now, in its eyes, you are nothing more than an extension of me.'

'Then get one of these to take it off.' Kimberley demanded as she rose from her seat.

'It's not that simple.' John hushed as he took hold of her hand to stop her from moving. 'This isn't something as simple as asking the nearest stranger to take it off.'

'How bad is it, having just one of them on?'

'As you saw in the Nuthall, i can still share memories, that's not changed. The rest is just harder to maintain and control.'

'What are we going to do no?'

'Honestly?' John scanned the room again as a drunken group burst through the fire door behind them, shouting and staggering around. 'I'm not sure. There are so many unanswered questions. I can't shake the feeling the Society is building up to something.'

Kimberley was jolted forward as one of the drunk men crashed into the back of her chair. Pinned to the table by the dead weight of the man, John was up in a flash and ripped the staggering man away from the table.

'Mind where's you're going.' John snapped as he pushed the unsteady man away.

'No harm, mate. Just an accident.' The man raised his hands up in mock surrender as John dismissed him.

'We should go.'

Offering her a hand, John hoisted Kimberley from her seat and they made for the exit. Pushing through the crowds, John felt Kimberley pulling at his arm as they moved.

'I don't feel right.' Kimberley slurred as her knees went from beneath her.

Catching her, John dropped to his knees and looked into her eyes. To any onlookers, Kimberley was a drunk woman who had had a few too many drinks, but John knew different. Knowing they hadn't touched a drop, John watched as her eyes rolled into her head and she went limp in his arms. Scanning the crowds, it all made sense as his attention settled on the rowdy group of drunk men who had burst through the fire escape. No longer unsteady on their feet, the four men's attention was now squarely fixed on John.

'How about we shroud this from the masses?' The Revenant's voice hissed as it stepped through the fire escape behind the four men.

Without warning, the room fell deathly silent as all the patrons suddenly froze in place. Knowing what was happening, John lowered Kimberley to the ground and checked he could feel the breath from her parted lips as he readied himself for the fight. As the Revenant pointed its spindly hand, he felt the familiar numbness where the tarnished blade had pierced his skin. Seeing the memory of their encounter in the burning underground station, John cast the thought aside. Ignoring the unsettling feeling, John once again removed the Moon Blade from his back and prepared himself for the inevitable fight.

'You would do well to simply surrender.' The Revenant warned as the four accompanying men flanked out either side of him. 'There is no escape for you.'

'Who said anything about escape?'

'Even better.'

Despite the dampening bracelet, John mustered all the control he could and flipped himself up into the air and onto the ceiling above the frozen crowds. Using it to his advantage, John sprinted the length of the roof before dropping beside one of the accompanying men. The fight between them was furious, each of the four men doing their best to overpower John as the Revenant stood back and watched. Seeing the amusement on the demonic creature's face only fuelled his grim determination. With ease, John disarmed the nearest of the men and turned his attention to the next. Keeping his attention on the Revenant, John seemed to almost casually despatch two of the four men before one of them landed a blow against John's shoulder.

Feeling the solid blow from the hammerhead weapon, the impact spun John on the spot as he came to a stop against the wall of the pub. Enraged by the sudden attack, John caught the follow up blow and easily snapped the man's arm with a sickening *crunch*. As the man's yelp echoed around the vaulted ceiling of the silent pub, John returned his attention to the Revenant.

'Are you going to fight me?' John snarled as he pushed the injured man aside. 'Or are you just going to stand there?'

'You're not a threat to me.'

Enraged by the dismissive reply, John surged forward and that was his undoing. Having fuelled his passion, the Revenant had done enough to blind John to the stealthy attack from the remaining man. As John bounded towards the creature, the man attacked. This was no attempt to render John immobile with the hammer-like weapon, instead the man made a simple move that ended everything. Throwing his arms out in fornt of him, reaching for the Revenant, John stopped dead in his tracks as the man slapped the second dampening bracelet on John's wrist.

Skidding to a stop, John felt his connection with his powers evaporate in an instant. The feeling of being submerged in water washed over him as his senses recoiled back to a level of normality and the world somehow took a dulled appearance to him. Staring down at the two intricate silver bracelets, John did not see the smile of success painted on the Revenant's face.

'That was always going to be your undoing.' The Revenant oozed as it moved to stand in front of him. 'For all your strength, your gifts, you remain absorbed in their world. For that, you will always be weaker than you should be.'

'Coward.'

Knocking the plague doctor mask from his face with a punch, the revenant stamped on the discarded leather mask as it landed by his feet. Unable to hide the defeat from his expression, John chanced a glance back at Kimberley as the remaining man hoisted her from the ground.

'I'd care less about her, and more about yourself.' The Revenant hushed in his ear. 'And I am no coward. I just know my place and my mission.'

'And what is that? What is your mission for the Society?'

'I would have thought that was obvious,' The creature replied between mocking laughter. 'I'm to bring you to them, alive. Well, not exactly alive, but as you are.'

'To what end?'

'All good things to those who wait.'

Before he could offer some witty retort, the Revenant crashed its elbow into his temple and unconsciousness washed over him. No longer protected by his heightened senses, there was nothing John could do to fight back the sea of darkness and silence that consumed him. Dropping to the ground, his last sight was of Kimberley being carried over the man's shoulder as he moved away through the frozen crowds of party-goers and patrons. Cursing himself silently, John watched the world fade to black and waited for the inevitable prison of his memories to return.

This was a state of consciousness he was all too familiar with. Severed from anything more than the exploration of his own memories, John knew he was once again powerless and incapable of fighting back. Whereas his incarceration in the Nuthall had begun by choice, soon evolving into a forced imprisonment, there was no choice in his current predicament. Hearing the echoing voices of his past calling to him, John had no idea how he was moved from the pub, or in fact where they were taking him.

14

THE LEY MAN

John and Kimberley remained blissfully unaware of their brief journey from The Ten Bells to Shoreditch. The streets were already alive with the throng of masked partygoers for the Blood Moon Festival. Navigating the back streets, the unremarkable grey van turned onto New Inn Broadway and pulled to the curb beside a rusted iron gate. The driver, a faceless man whose eyes could be seen above the cloth face mask, jumped out of the idling van and approached the gate. With no view beyond, he rattled his fist on the metal sheet welded to the bars and took a step back.

The gate sat beneath a weathered sandstone block that read CURTAIN STREET SCHOOL, the lettering long faded from exposure to the elements. To most, the entry was nothing more than a relic of a long forgotten school, but to those who knew, it was more. The site of the old Holywell Priory, little remained of the foundations or impressive priory among the new buildings of London. Hearing footsteps behind the gate, the man waited for the locks to move aside and the heavy gate to part with the wall.

'Were you seen?' The voice pressed from behind the same mask the driver wore.

'No. But we should get them below ground before the streets are teeming with people.'

In a matter of minutes, Kimberley and John were carried from the back of the van and through the narrow gate into the walled complex of the former school. Now home of the London College of Fashion, the plethora of windows overlooking the gated entrance appeared dark and empty. Ignoring the fact they may be seen, the group made their way along the side of the college building. Reaching a nondescript set of stairs leading down into the pavement, the group did not pause and quickly disappeared below ground level.

Following the snaking tunnels beneath the school, it was clear they were remnants of the old priory that had once stood on the site. Carved out of the sandstone, the tunnels were lit only by flickering torches as far they could see.

'Is it really happening?' The driver huffed as he adjusted his grip on the makeshift stretcher holding John. 'After all this time, will the prophecy be realised?'

'That's what is being whispered in the temple.'

The sound of voices carried along the tunnel towards them. Quickening their pace, the group turned the corner and found their path blocked by two familiar figures.

'Thank you brothers,' Diana offered as she pointed towards an open door to the side of the tunnel. 'You may place him in there.'

'And the woman?'

'We will take her from here.' Qamar answered.

Lowering Kimberley to the ground, the four men carrying John made quick work of placing him in the dark cell, closing the door as they left.

'You may resume your duties.' Diana dismissed as she peered through the barred opening in the reinforced wooden door.

'As you wish.' Taking their leave, the gaggle of masked members promptly left Diana, Qamar and Kimberley alone in the corridor. Peering into the dark cell, the narrow square of light illuminated John's face. Seeing him motionless, Diana feared the Revenant had done more than render him unconscious. At last, after what felt like an age to her, John rolled his head and weakly opened his eyes as if sensing her gaze.

'That's right, you're back where you belong. Under my watchful eye.' Diana hissed through the opening as John's senses remained somewhere between awake and asleep.

'I'm not sure I approve of your choice to bring her here. We could have been done with her at the hotel. There were men positioned to end her involvement.'

'Indulge me.'

'And your curious motherly whims?' Qamar snapped as he stalked away.

'She still has a part to play in this.' Diana protested as she stalked after Qamar.

'I struggle to believe that. To me, it's nothing more than a delay tactic for what will be an inevitable end to your pet.'

Their argument continued as they returned to the privacy of the crypt. Once again the fireplace was filled with raging fire that sent the shadows dancing around the room. Now stained by the sacrifices of blood from the curious ritual of the Full Moon Society members, the once pale stone coffin was now crimson. Blood had pooled at the coffin's base and the crystal burned heart shimmered in the firelight, now also stained with blood. Diana could immediately taste the coppery blood in the air and took a moment to compose herself as Qamar stormed to his seat in front of the fire.

'You're missing the point.' Diana snapped as she slammed her hand on the wooden table. 'His mind is in a case of flux right now. You forget I know exactly how this works with him, I am the *only* one who knows.'

'I don't care where his mind is. What matters is the fact his body is here.'

'Are you so foolish and blind to the prophecy's meaning?' Diana scoffed as she looked across at Qamar.

'You forget your place in the Society.'

'Pecking order and rituals will mean nothing once the prophecy is realised.' Diana corrected. 'Until that happens, you can look down on me from your pretty pedestal. But remember who it is that has brought him here for the Blood Moon.'

'You've fulfilled your task.' Qamar conceded, his tone laced with disdain. 'But you're still beneath me.'

'Beneath, beside...I don't care. What I care about is resurrecting him.' Diana pointed to the blood-soaked coffin. 'That is all I have wanted for as long as I can remember.'

Diana's voice trailed off for a moment as she admired the ornate decorations etched into the surfaces of the coffin. Drenched in blood, the shadows of each design looked deeper and the details even more defined. There was something almost romantic about the curious mix of blood and pale stone. Feeling Qamar's gaze on her back, Diana peeled her attention away from the coffin and turned to look at him.

'We have the burnt jewel, as you can see.' Qamar pointed towards the shimmering heart. 'We have the hell demons throne, and its rightful occupant in the coffin there.'

'And so, as the prophecy speaks, both twins will meet a fight.'

'I'm aware of the meaning. Why do you think he is here?'

'Both were born from deviations of messengers, the Ripper from the Dark Angel and the Raven from Death's. All that remains is the ultimate sacrifice to ensure our Ripper's ascension.'

'Their fight will finally open the seat of power. I know this.'

'And if John is trapped in a world of memories and imagination, how can he fight?'

'The Ripper, once released, can simply rip the life from him and be done.'

'Despite your own lack of honour, that is not the way of things. We must honour his sacrifice in battle.'

'And your little bitch can ensure that?'

'She is the catalyst for his powers. With the dampening bracelets in place, he will lose his connection and be nothing more than a lost soul. We needed them to bring him here, but he will need to be revived the moment we call the Ripper back into this world.'

'Could he best the Ripper again?'

'Yes.' Diana conceded, seeing the immediate concern on Qamar's face. 'But his powers are not immediate. Bringing them back at the right moment will see the Ripper's victory.'

'You're playing a dangerous game.' Qamar declared as he toyed with a dagger in his hand. 'We risk giving the Raven what he wants in finally vanquishing the Ripper to the afterlife.'

'It is the prophecy.' Diana corrected. 'Regardless of our pre-ferred route, this is the way the fates have proclaimed it must happen. You know that as much as I do!'

'We are so close,' Qamar groaned as he pressed the tip of the blade into his wrist. 'And yet we teeter on the edge of failure, our fate decided by a battle of powers we will never possess.'

'The festival is tonight. The gathering will provide us the souls for the Ripper's army *when* he claims the demons throne.'

'Aren't you afraid of failing?'

'I've come too far to fall at the last hurdle.'

'We, we have come too far, Diana.'

'Shall I summon the Ley Man?'

Qamar kept his attention on the dagger as a trickle of blood traced around his wrist to drip onto the floor by his feet. Knowing she was right did not make his decision any easier. It still felt risky, even after everything they had done to honour the prophecy, the efforts to bring everything to bear on a night when the Ripper would be afforded the greatest chance of success. Despite his retlcence, Qamar knew the only course of action was the one they were on. With an almost dismissive wave of his hand, he turned to face Diana.

'Summon the Ley Man.' Qamar offered with a deep sigh. 'We chose tonight for a reason. Our predecessors chose this site for the same reason. We would be foolish to not to harness the power of a Blood Moon and the Ley Lines.'

'It shall be done.'

Excusing herself from the room, Diana left Qamar alone in front of the roaring fire. Sensing her presence within the flames, Qamar searched the fire for Amber's face.

'I know you've been listening.' Qamar declared as he stuck the dagger into the arm of his chair. 'Is there something you wish to add?'

'I appreciate your nervousness, but this is what is needed to resurrect my messenger.' Amber's face moved int he fire. 'You should be proud of what you have achieved.'

'I am.'

'But?'

'I fear we've come this far only to fail in the final stages.' Qamar could not hide his nervousness.

'Do you trust the prophecy?'

'Of course.'

'Then allow it to run its course.' Amber soothed from inside the fireplace. 'You have aligned all the pieces like a master chessman, do not let fear falter you now.'

'And our reward?'

'Life eternal.' Amber hissed from within the flames. 'You're place will be secured. You have done your society proud.'

Amber's face faded from the flames leaving Qamar alone in the silent crypt. Hearing footsteps in the distance, he knew Diana would return with the Ley Man in tow. Taking a moment to compose himself, he knew the ritual that would follow had already begun with the spilling of the society member's blood on the coffin behind him. There was no denying his sense of pride of what *he* had achieved. Although Diana had played her part, a significant one he acknowledged, it had been his lifelong honour to sit as the head of the Full Moon Society for almost three decades. Everything they had achieved, had been instigated by him.

Casting aside any doubts his fearful brain created, Qamar took a deep breath and turned in time to see the robed and masked Ley Man stalk into the room, followed by Diana.

'Am I to believe the ritual is to enter the final stages?' The man's voice carried a thick South African accent.

'It has.'

'Then we should summon the bearers and raise the coffin into the Main Chamber.'

'See to it.' Qamar instructed as he lifted from the chair. 'Diana and I shall prepare for the ceremony.'

Taking his leave, the Ley Man disappeared out of the door leaving the pair of them alone.

'I can't believe it's finally happening.' Diana struggled to hide her excitement as she spoke. 'Everything has led us to this moment.'

'That it has. We shall see the Ley Man channel the power of this place and watch as the Ripper takes his rightful place.'

'When shall we bring *him* to the chamber?'

'When life returns to the Ripper's body, then we will present the sacrifice of the Raven to him.'

15

JOHN'S HOME

'Hello?' John's voice carried through the open door and into the building he had avoided in his memories.

He knew this place too well, even when he had returned with Kimberley to see his wife and son emerging from the house, he knew he would not step in. Standing at the threshold, he felt different this time, somehow as if the house was calling to him, inviting him in.

'Excuse me?' A woman's voice replied from somewhere in the shadows. 'Who is it?'

Seeing her silhouette, John felt his heart swim with emotions he had long buried in the darkest pit of his stomach. Hearing her soft voice, John knew how she would react and quickly turned from the door and launched down the steps.

'Wrong house, sorry.' John blurted as the woman arrived in the doorway.

'I know that voice.' John froze as she spoke. 'It's a voice I've longed to hear a thousand times, but even in the dark he never answers.'

'You must have me confused with someone else,' John croaked. 'Sorry for disturbing you.'

John knew how delicate his presence was in his memories at the best of times, risking disrupting the balance by speaking to his wife was more than dangerous. Steeling himself, John made to move but stopped when he felt a soft hand on his shoulder.

'It is you, isn't it?'

Frozen, unable to move as her delicate hand held his shoulder, John needed to run. Rooted to the spot, he felt her tug on his shoulder and force him to face her. Unsure if he would have ever resisted her touch, John allowed himself to turn and face his wife. Instantly the world muted around him as he drank in her beauty, a face he had not seen up close for far too long.

'How is this possible?' She asked, placing her hand to his cheek.

'It isn't.' John struggled to keep his composure as he felt her fingers explore his face, somehow testing if what she was seeing was real. 'I'm not who you think I am.'

'I would know that face, that voice, anywhere.'

Before he could reply, she moved closer and pressed her lips to his. Swallowed by her touch, John wrapped his arms around his wife and pulled her closer. Feeling her body against his, he realised how much he had missed her. All those years of buried emotion overflowed inside, and he felt tears form in his eyes.

'I've missed you, so much.' John's voice quivered as he pulled his face away. 'Oh Ann, you have no idea how long I've waited for that kiss. But this is wrong.'

Pulling away, John longed not to let her go, but knew he had to. Nothing about this was real, and wallowing in his past was not healthy.

'Where have you been?'

'Here.' John replied, sensing movement in the doorway behind Ann.

'It's been years,' Ann offered as she too sensed the movement at the door. 'He'll probably not recognise you.'

'Don't...' John pleaded, but it was too late as Ann called his son's name.

Hearing the gentle voice of his son, John was frozen and fought every urge to turn around. Knowing how his boy would look, the innocent shimmer to his wide eyes and perfectly parted brown hair, he had enough memories to hold his son close. Fighting back a sudden surge of tears, John looked beyond Ann at the street behind them as if fighting to acknowledge what was happening.

'He's waiting for you.' Ann hushed as she moved to whisper in his ear. 'He's waited a long time for his dad, don't deny him now.'

Forcing him to turn around, John couldn't say he honestly resisted his wife moving him. Keeping his attention to the towering townhouse, he counted the chimneys before moving slowly down the soot-stained frontage and at last to the open door. Standing in the doorway was the boy John had never met, his own son. Having watched him grow from the shadows, observing at a distance had been a more painful torture than turning away and doing his best to forget what had been stolen from him.

'This is your dad.' Ann declared from behind.

'You shouldn't have told him.' John snapped as he snatched his head around to look at his wife. 'I won't be able to stay.'

Knowing the world would come crumbling down around him and the contents of his memory turn on him, he prepared for a fight. Calling the plague doctor mask to his face, the leather could not form as Ann pressed her hand to his face, stopping it manifesting.

'You won't be needing that.' She soothed, locking gazes with him. 'This isn't the place you think it is, we are not here as your enemy.'

'What is this place then, if not my memory?'

'This is your home, John Smith, and we are your family.'

Scanning the street, John expected to see the streets filled with the figures from his memories staring at him, ready to attack. Instead, the world remained unchanged around him, nobody paid him the slightest attention save his son in the doorway whose face was awash with concern and confusion.

'Dad?'

Having never heard the words uttered from his son's mouth, John's legs collapsed beneath him. All at once every emotion and sensation he had bottled and ignored came washing over him. Gasping for breath, despite not needing it, John looked to the heavens and recalled every moment he had watched his family from the shadows. Ever aware of the fact this wasn't real, there was no denying the surge of emotions that overcame him.

'Come speak to him.' Ann urged, encouraging the petrified boy from the doorway.

'I know you're not..' John feared completing his sentence as Ann dropped to his side.

'We are as real as you want us to be.' She pressed her hand to his chest for a moment. 'What does your heart tell you?'

'I have no heart.' John protested, and the it happened.

Beyond all realms of possibility, John *heard* the beating of his own heart in his ears. Unused to the *thump-thump* sound of his pounding heart, John ripped himself away. As the panic set in, the sound boomed louder in his head until it felt like his heartbeat was all-consuming and somehow all around him. Fighting to make sense of what was happening, John felt his body shut down as he collapsed to the floor.

As darkness washed over him, the last impossible sound John heard was the thumping of his heart in his ears.

'You're home, John.' Ann's voice echoed somewhere in the distance as all his senses shut down.

When John awoke, his eyes opened and scanned the curious room that surrounded him. Recognising nothing of the dark decoration and paintings that adorned the walls, John sat bolt upright in bed and felt the room swim around him. Calming himself as best he could, John waited for the sliver of light between the curtains to stop spinning before daring to move again.

'Is it true?' A curious young voice hushed from the room's corner. 'Are you really my dad?'

'Where's Ann,' John croaked. 'I mean, where's your mum.'

'She's waiting downstairs,' the young voice replied. 'She said I should get her when you woke up.'

'You should do as she asked.'

'Not yet.' His answer was filled with a surprising adultness. 'I want to ask you something.'

'You should get your mum.'

'Won't you answer me one question?'

'Go on.'

At last, John saw movement in the direction of the voice and watched as his son moved in front of the curtains. Silhouetted by the narrow beam of light, John could see nothing of his son's face as he stood looking at him in the bed. Unnerved by the boy's reluctance to fetch his wife, John waited for the question. Deep down, John's nervousness did not come from the boy's silence, but from the fact he knew what the question was going to be. Despite everything, his son was a boy who had been abandoned by his father, he knew he had a right to know why.

'Where did you go, and why did you leave me?'

'Didn't your mum tell you what happened?'

'She said you died.' John was about to reply but his son cut him short. 'But now you're here, I know that was a lie.'

'It's complicated.'

'Was it because of me?' His son's voice quivered as he spoke, fighting to hold back the emotion. 'I was only a baby when you left, was there something wrong with me?'

'Not at all.'

'Didn't you want me then, is that what it was?' Despite the shadows, John could tell the boy was crying. 'Was I the bastard son you never wanted?'

'I loved your mother,' John protested. 'And I loved you. Had there been any other way, I would have come back to you.'

'Then why didn't you?'

'It's not easy to explain.'

'Don't you think he deserves an explanation?'

'What?'

'Your son, don't you think he deserves an explanation?'

The room grew darker as the shadows extended from the corner where his son had come from. Scanning the darkness, John called to his powers but felt no response.

'Who are you?'

'You know.' The voice changed, morphing from the softness of a boy's voice to a sinister drawl John immediately recognised.

'You're dead.' John snapped as he launched from the bed and scanned for any sign of the Ripper. 'I killed you twice.'

'You trapped me, once.'

'And I ripped your dead heart from your chest!' John spat.

'This heart?'

Before he could answer, the bloodstained crystal heart landed on the bed by his side. Leaving a smear of bloodstains as it came to rest beside the pillow, John struggled to make sense of *how*. Eyeing the shimmering heart, John watched as the shadows within the room expanded and spread towards him. Feeling their presence around, John backed away towards the door and fumbled with the handle at his back. Finding the battered doorknob, he yanked open the door and launched out of the room.

'Ann?' John screamed as he ran down the staircase.

It took five turns before John realised the stairs were not leading anywhere. Moving to the banister, he looked down to see nothing but darkness. Craning his neck upwards, he saw the same never-ending spiral of stairs leading up, with no sign of the bedroom he had escaped from.

'What is this place?' John hollered as he leapt down to the next level down. 'Where is my wife?'

'You know where you are.' The mocking voice of the Ripper offered as it came into view on the next level down. 'You're with me now.'

'How are you here?' John gasped as he backed away. 'Your heart is on the bed up there, without it, you shouldn't even exist.'

'Because, my dear boy.' The Ripper offered as it nonchalantly sauntered up the steps towards him. 'That isn't my heart. It was the heart of one of my kind who could bend you to our will.'

'To your will?'

'The prophecy,' the Ripper hissed as the chalked letters etched on the Victorian door appeared on the wall in front of John.

'That's not your prophecy.' John scoffed as he re-read the all too familiar passage, **the Juwes are the men that will not be blamed for nothing**.

'This breadcrumb has always been your beacon.' The Ripper teased as the letters began to dance on the wall. 'Always an anchor to your past, a reminder of what your future held.'

'Speak sense.'

'These words are more than a simple message. Your world believed them to declare a man's intention and motivation.'

'A narrative released to appease the masses in a time of fear and frenzy.'

'But also a beacon to those within the Society, that the prophecy had begun.'

Offering no more words, the letters within Jack The Ripper's infamous passage moved around their positions on the wall until they came to rest in a form that John recognised. With every letter accounted for, John realised how blind he had been to everything and how easily he had been manipulated by the very things he had sworn to destroy. His oath to Death meant nothing, as the words settled in place and once again attached themselves to the wall.

'A burnt jewel, a demons throne, both twins will meet a fight.' John gasped as he read the re-ordered passage.

'That jewel lies on your bed and the throne awaits.'

'And the twins?' John pressed despite suspecting he knew the answer already.

'My brother, we were both born of dark magic beyond the realm of the living. Neither of us legitimate in the order, we are brothers of chaos.'

As the Ripper made his declaration, the staircase collapsed around him and a new world took shape around them.

16

———— ⚬ ————

ONE LAST OFFER

Kimberley found herself alone in the subterranean crypt where Qamar and Diana had spent their time in conversation with Amber through the fire. Although the fireplace was now dark, the smell of smoke still hung in the air. Scuffing the charred logs, she had been left alone since their captors had deposited John in his cell. Secured by a large wooden door, there was no chance of escape and she had set about exploring the curious room.

Ignoring the fireplace, Kimberley moved to the enormous bookshelves and scanned the spines. Very few were labelled, and those that were looked to be written in Latin or other languages she did not recognise. Picking one out at random, Kimberley pulled it free and admired the worn leather cover before opening it.

'You'd do well to understand what's written in there.' Qamar declared as he stepped through the now open door.

Catching a glimpse of the corridor outside the room, it surprised her to see a hive of activity as people moved with haste outside. Seeing Diana follow Qamar, she slammed the book shut and tossed it onto the table.

'Have more respect.' Qamar boomed as he moved to retrieve the discarded book from the table. 'Some of these are priceless.'

'Oops.'

'She's yours to entertain yourself with.' Qamar snapped as he brushed off the cover and gently replaced it into the gap Kimberley had left in the bookshelf. 'I'm tired of her.'

'Be sure to close the door on your way out.' Kimberley offered, seeing the well-dressed man tense as she spoke.

'You shouldn't be so quick to offend him.' Diana warned as she offered for Kimberley to take a seat at the table. 'I've already had a hard enough time convincing him not to use you in the sacrifice ceremony.'

'And you expect me to be grateful about that?'

'Must you be so insolent all the time?' Diana groaned as she slid into the seat opposite. 'There's so much you could learn from us, if you simply opened your ears and stopped pretending you aren't curious.'

'I'm not as curious as you'd like me to be.' Kimberley replied, scanning the curious room. 'I've seen a lot through John's memories.'

'There is no John!' Diana snapped and tossed her coin across the table to Kimberley. 'It's a foolish notion that consumed the creature he should have become.'

'The Raven?'

'What pitiful connection he clung onto almost cost us the prophecy.' Diana spat as Kimberley looked at the face of the coin in front of her. 'When he was given his duty, it should have been his everything. John Smith died on the eighth of November, he should have accepted that fate.'

'It makes him human.'

'He isn't human, and you would do well to remember that.'

'He's more human than you.' Kimberley saw a flicker of hurt on Diana's face that was quickly hidden.

'You really have fallen under his spell, haven't you?'

'Better than falling under yours.' Kimberley's defiance was wearing thin with Diana. 'But, I'll humour you for a moment. Since you clearly want to do your villain monologue at me.'

'Enough!' Diana slammed her hands on the table, sending the coin clattering to the stone floor at Kimberley's feet. 'The Raven never achieved his true potential and never accepted his connection to the realm between our worlds. When he surrendered himself into the Nuthall, he was lost and broken. I have devoted everything to bringing him back to where he needed to be.'

'Why? If it's his job to banish your little army of Revenants and Rippers, why would you want him back where he belongs?'

'Life is like that coin at your feet. There's a reason one side is empty and the other shows the face of a fallen demon.' Diana watched as Kimberley retrieved the coin. 'Life is always built on balance, co-existing powers, and that is what he is.'

'You believe all this, don't you?'

'So do you!' Diana quipped. 'I can see it in your eyes. Despite everything, you know what I'm saying is true. Without The Raven, there is no prophecy, only with him can we reach the end.'

'What end?'

Kimberley watched as Diana fidgeted in her seat, suddenly the flow of gloating information had stumbled and a different expression appeared on her face. Unsure of what to make of the sudden change, Kimberley dropped her attention to the coin and took in the detail of the embossed demon's head on the face that looked up at her. Feeling the etched eyes somehow watching her, Kimberley flipped the coin over and placed it back onto the table.

'We all have our own reasons for allying with the Full Moon Society. For Qamar, it is his promise of immortality.'

'And yours?'

'Freedom.' Diana rose from her seat and stalked along the table to retrieve her coin. 'Without his sacrifice, the prophecy cannot be fulfilled. It was you who brought him back from the prison of his own mind. And for that, I thank you.'

'Go to hell.'

'I've already been.' Diana replied as she snatched the coin from the table and stalked towards the door. 'They'll fetch you in a few moments, I'd hate for you to miss this.'

'How long?' Kimberley replied as Diana ripped open the door. 'How long have you played me? Since I applied for access to your hospital?'

'Long before then my dear.' Diana offered a twisted smirk as she looked at Kimberley. 'We have been controlling your life since your childhood.'

'How?'

'We've always known who you were to him. Despite Qamar's reluctance, I knew you would be the key to his return. Every decision you've ever made was only an illusion, you were always going to end up here.'

'You're lying.'

'Believe what you want. But, for your service, the Society thanks you, I thank you.'

Leaving Kimberley to make sense of her words, Diana disappeared through the door and closed it behind her. Despite all her self-control and look of calmness, the moment the wooden door shut, Kimberley broke down. As tears streamed down her face, she threw her head back and looked towards the ceiling of the subterranean crypt.

'He's going to need you, now more than ever.' The woman's voice echoed in her head, but Kimberley knew who it belonged to.

'You sent me back to find him, I saved him from the Ripper.'

'We saw.' Her voice was everywhere, but nowhere as Kimberley scanned the room.

'What happens if they kill him?'

'Then the barrier that restricts the movement of their kind, will be open.'

'There are already dozens of those things, I've seen so many Revenants and more.'

'But there is only ever one of him.'

'The Ripper?'

'Yes.'

'What is he?'

'The most dangerous of creatures. They are born from Sub Terra itself, soulless and empty shells.'

'Sub Terra?'

'Hell, or what you would think of hell.' Ann's voice explained, bringing Kimberley's attention back to the empty fireplace. 'That's why it feeds on the living, drinking their souls to maintain its existence.'

'Hasn't John already banished him twice?'

'Only once,' the voice explained as the fire crackled back to life. 'He trapped the defeated Ripper in the Zassuru, but the second, the one you saw, was another of its kind.'

'How could that be though, you said there's only ever been one.'

'One at a time. The dark magic that restricts what Death can do, also controls the actions of the Dark Angel.'

'You've lost me.'

Footsteps echoed outside the door and suddenly Kimberley felt an unseen hand on her shoulder. Hearing Ann's voice as a whisper in her ear, she could almost picture the Victorian woman poised over her, speaking so only she could hear. Feeling the heat of her breath on her neck, Kimberley couldn't help but shudder as Ann spoke.

'See the damage a single Ripper has done. With the original banished, they released another, an infant in comparison, and with its death opened the door to the rebirth of the original Ripper. If he's not already awake, he will be. John has one chance to stop him.'

'How am I supposed to help?'

'That's for you to find out. But know this, if John falls, they have won. This world will become their feeding ground.'

Before Ann could speak again, the door burst open and three figures clad in crimson robes stalked over the threshold.

'You will be restrained.' A gruff voice boomed from beneath its hood. 'There will be no argument.'

As the robed figure approached, Kimberley knew she had no choice and held out her hands so they could be bound. Having no clue what was going to happen, she scanned the room one last time but found no sign of Ann, only the tendrils of flame snaking over the charred logs in the fireplace. Leaving the room, flanked by two of the robed guards, Kimberley was promptly ushered along the corridor.

'Don't bother trying to speak with him, he can't hear you.' Her escort scoffed as they moved past the open door to John's cell.

In the fleeting glimpse she had, Kimberley saw John laid on the floor, his face uncovered from the plague doctor mask and two other robed figures in the process of lifting him onto a gurney. Desperate to help, any thought of resisting was halted as the binds around her wrists were yanked forward, pulling off balance.

'I'm coming.'

'The Brother Qamar has seen fit to let you, an outsider, observe the rituals.' There was an obvious disdain in the gruff voice.

'You don't agree?'

'What I think is of little consequence.' The figure stopped and turned to face her. 'But I tell you this. If you do anything to disrupt the proceedings, I will kill you myself and face the consequences with Sister Diana.'

Not given a chance to reply, they set off again and Kimberley was led up the spiral staircase to the higher levels of the curious underground temple complex. Reaching the top of the staircase, the shallowness of the steps had left her strangely out of breath. Given a moment to compose herself, she couldn't help but admire the enormous statue of a mythical creature sat beside the open door leading into the main chamber.

Fighting her childhood memories to recognise the creature, her concentration was shattered as she was pulled through the open door and her attention fell to the masses of robed figures filling in the chamber. With the inverted dome roof, her attention naturally fell to the raised platform where Qamar and Diana now stood. At the foot of the platform, she could see a disturbingly bloodstained stone coffin that appeared to be the focus of everyone's attention.

'Close the doors.' Qamar's voice echoed across the chamber. 'We shall begin the ritual and set in motion the final stages of the prophecy.'

No longer of concern to anyone but the man that had bound her wrists, Kimberley watched as the doors to the chamber were secured behind her. As a hefty wooden bar was slid into position, she knew there would be no chance of lifting it and escaping on her own. Scanning the see of shadowed hoods, she wondered who was hiding beneath the robes and suspected there would be many faces she would not have expected to see among the sea of demon worshippers.

As Qamar spoke again, the chamber was plunged into darkness and all Kimberley could hear was her own breath in the silence.

17

RIPPER REBORN

A steady beat of drums reverberated around the chamber and all eyes fell to the bloodstained stone coffin. Unable to see the drummers, hidden somewhere in the shadows at the far side of the room, she couldn't help but feel her heart beating in time to the rhythmic *thump-thump* of the drums. The heavy bass drowned out Qamar's words as she recited a ritual she was not familiar with. Zoning her attention in on the coffin, her senses could only compute the gruesome sight and the pounding drums as she moved between the rows of robed figures, edging closer to the coffin.

Reaching the limit of how far her escort would allow, she felt his arm on her shoulder, stopping her a handful of metres away from the coffin. Overcome with curiosity, she admired the intricate carvings across the faces of the coffin. The mix of dried blood and pale stone complimented one another in a sickening way. Kimberley could clearly see where the blood had followed the channels carved into the stone, accentuating the details of the lettering and faces on the stone.

'No further,' her escort hissed in her ear. 'You can watch from here.'

Offering no response, Kimberley watched as the drums fell silent and the light within the chamber dimmed.

'We stand on the cusp of the prophecy's realisation.' Qamar announced as he descended from his platform, followed by Diana. 'You all stand here, devoted to realising the prophecy.'

'We do.' The chorus of voices responded in unison. 'We stand as one in the face of power.'

Everything was so sickeningly rehearsed that Kimberley felt the wonder of the moment disappear a little.

'We gather before the Fallen Dark Angel that is our Ripper. With our blood oath, he shall rise.'

'He shall rise.' The crowd chanted.

'But the prophecy speaks too of the fight of twins.' Qamar shifted his attention to the far side of the chamber where John was being wheeled into the room atop the gurney. 'We have caged The Raven, and present him now as the Ripper rises.'

Kimberley watched as Qamar and Diana positioned themselves at either end of the stone coffin. She could have heard a pin drop as the gurney came to a stop beside the bloodstained coffin. Watching the escorts back away, only Qamar, Diana, a motionless John, and the coffin remained in the room's centre.

'Get up.' Kimberley hissed under her breath as she saw John's eyes dancing from side-to-side beneath his eyelids. 'They need you.'

'Quiet.' Her escort spat and jabbed his elbow into her ribs.

Removing their own blades, Qamar and Diana moved in unison, their actions deliberate and theatrical for all in the chamber to see. Raising their left arms into the air, both peeled back the sleeve of their gowns and pressed the tip of the blade in the crook of their elbow. The pair silently and calmly cut their skin from elbow to wrist, skirting their arteries to show their trust and commitment to the ritual. Lowering their arms, both allowed the steady stream of blood to pool in the palm of their hands before looking to one another and placing their bloodied palm onto the stone lid of the coffin.

The moment their hands touched the stone, the drums began again, and all attention was transfixed on the pair.

'We spill our blood as our brothers and sisters.' Diana declared as she lifted her hand free, leaving the bloodstain handprint on the stone.

'We gather the vessels above for the Ripper's victory and the removal of the barriers of old.' Qamar hissed as he too removed his hand from the stone.

'Power shall be restored,' Diana continued. 'We present the twin for your sacrifice.'

As they fell silent, the drums continued until a new sound echoed around the chamber. Matching the beat of the drums, this sound was more hollow and closer. Knowing what it was, Kimberley hoped she was wrong, as her attention fell to the stone lid of the coffin that now *moved* with each beat of the drum. As the drums trailed away, the rhythmic sound continued, and there was no denying it was coming from the coffin in front of her.

At last, the coffin lid propelled into the air and came crashing to the ground beside it, smashing into four pieces on the stone floor. Instinctively, everyone in the room took a step back as a thin cloud of dust billowed over the lip of the open coffin. Kimberley was captivated, holding her breath, as a hand in a black glove rose above the coffin's edge. Wrapping its fingers over the edge, Kimberley watched as an enormous figure lifted itself up through the thin cloud of dust and stood tall in front of them.

The Ripper did not unfold from the coffin. Even between the swirling dust, Kimberley could see the Ripper growing from the coffin. As its torso and legs took shape, so too did the top hat on its head as it turned to look at Qamar who stood awestruck.

'You bring me back?' The Ripper's voice crackled.

'We did.' Qamar answered and retrieved the crimson crystal heart from the bag at his waist. 'And we bring you this.'

Holding out the crystal heart, Kimberley could see the look of excitement on the charred face. As the dust settled, she could make out every inch of terrifying detail of the Ripper. The Ripper's clothes looked to be burned and discoloured while its flesh was cracked, each crack shimmering like the heat within was trying to break free. What caught Kimberley's attention the most, beside his enormous frame, were the lifeless red eyes that stared at her across the room.

'She is his blood.' The Ripper snarled as it sniffed the air while stepping out of the coffin. 'But she will not be enough to sacrifice and honour the prophecy.'

'You're right, 'Diana continued. 'That is why we have brought you him.'

The Ripper stopped mid-step and turned his attention back to Diana and Qamar. Looking beyond them, his attention fell to the gurney and John's lifeless form bound to it. Watching the evil smirk paint itself on its crooked face, The Ripper disregarded Kimberley and stalked back to the coffin. Reaching Qamar it snatched the crystal heart and turned around to face Kimberley.

'If she is of no use, why is she here?' The Ripper quizzed as it admired the many faces of shimmering crystal in its hand.

'We would see her embraced into the Society, should she see sense in your rebirth.'

'She will not turn.' The Ripper declared. 'His strength flows through her, waste no more time on her.'

Kimberley was about to speak when the impossible happened. Moving aside the burnt white shirt, The Ripper exposed its chest, and she watched as the skin peeled open to reveal the empty chest within him. Sickened by the sight, she forced herself to watch as The Ripper placed the crystal heart inside his own chest and waited for the burned flesh and bone to knit itself back over the hole he had created.

The Ripper's body twitched and convulsed, the bright light tracing between the cracks in his charred flesh pulsed and fizzled as the heart in its chest found its place.

'I am now a man, no longer an empty vessel.' He declared and raised his hands to the inverse domed ceiling. 'You have done well to realise the prophecy and bring me everything I need to claim my place on the demon throne.'

Stalking around the now empty coffin, The Ripper loomed over John and admired his motionless form bound to the table. Placing its blackened hand on John's chest, Kimberley could only watch as the resurrected demon toyed with John.

'You're a coward.' Kimberley yelled as Qamar offered the Moon Blade to The Ripper.

As the words left her lips, she felt a solid blow in her stomach that sent her doubling over. Her enraged escort was about to strike again when The Ripper's voice halted his movement.

'Bring her to me.'

Gasping for breath from the solid blow, Kimberley felt herself dragged across the cobbled floor and deposited on the far side of the coffin at The Ripper's feet. Looking up at the demon, she felt her heart skip a beat, being so close. Immediately her mind raced back to the world of the other Ripper's memories and knew how much darker this one's would be by the empty look in his lifeless eyes.

'She speaks out of turn.' Diana interjected as The Ripper took the blade. 'She is defiant, but worthy of our attention.'

'Enough.' Qamar snapped. 'Your obsession with keeping her safe is sickening. She is not your child. Let her fate be decided by The Ripper.'

'She speaks the truth.' The Ripper hissed as it teased the hooked Moon Blade over John's body, coming to settle on his throat. 'I am no coward, but you speak the truth. This is not the way of the prophecy.'

'The Raven must die. Only then can you claim your throne.' Qamar argued, his voice quivering with anger. 'We have amassed a thousand vessels for your army on the streets above.'

'You have done well.' The Ripper complimented as it toyed with the hooked blade across John's dead flesh. 'But the prophecy must be honoured.'

'It has,' Qamar boomed as he moved to take hold of the Moon Blade. 'You must end him and arise.'

To the room's surprise, The Ripper swiped his hand through the air, slamming it into the side of Qamar's face, sending him crashing to the floor. Stunned into silence, the man looked up at the Ripper and along the hooked blade that was now pointed in his direction. Quivering beneath The Ripper's venomous glare, Qamar fell silent.

'You speak of honouring the oath.' The Ripper began, addressing the cavernous room. 'And yet you ask me to fulfill the prophecy without honour?'

Stalking to the nearest row of robed disciples, The Ripper ripped off the hood and punched the Moon Blade through the unsuspecting man's chest sending a spray of blood on the row behind. Unflinching and unmoving, the surrounding disciples watched as The Ripper tore the young man's heart from his chest and the lifeless body crumpled to the floor at his feet.

Biting into the heart, The Ripper once again pulsed with veins of shimmering light until there was nothing left of the heart in his hands.

'A burnt jewel,' the gathered crowds chanted in chorus. 'A demon throne.'

'Both twins will meet a fight.' The Ripper completed the prophecy and launched through the air back towards John and the gurney.

Kimberley watched as The Ripper straddled over John. Removing his top hat, the demon leaned closer and whispered something into John's ear. The unheard words had a reaction as his eyes moved faster beneath his eyelids. Moving himself away, the Ripper turned to look at Kimberley as he raised the Moon Blade into the air and drove it down. Clamping her eyes shut, not wanting to see the spiteful execution, all she heard was Qamar's voice.

'What are you doing?'

'What I must.' the Ripper declared.

Kimberley only opened her eyes when she heard an impossible voice echo around the cavernous room.

'That probably wasn't your wisest move.' John declared and Kimberley opened her eyes to see John rise from the gurney and the plague doctor mask form itself over his face.

As the eyeholes took shape, Kimberley saw John's eyes and he offered her nothing more than a wink as his face disappeared.

'Both twins will meet a fight.' The Ripper boomed as he launched the gurney across the room and the gathered disciples scattered.

18

—— ◆ ——

BOTH TWINS MEET A FIGHT

A s the room emptied of the robed disciples, John pulled off the long coat and threw it over the open coffin. Smoothing the plague doctor mask to his face, he took a moment to collect his senses.

Reeling from being ripped back from the world of his own memories, John suppressed the swell of sadness that lingered in him at the fact he had lost his family, *again*. Aware that his connection to his powers were back, feeling the familiar tingle in his fingers, John called the escrima sticks into his open hands. Not recognising the cavernous room, his attention fell to Kimberley for a moment and the burly figure that remained behind her. Regaining his composure, John tested the weight of his wooden weapons in each hand before turning his masked head to face The Ripper.

'You know what this is?' The Ripper snarled, gripping the Moon Blade in one hand and a Liston Knife in the other.

'Your sad prophecy?'

'Exactly.'

Still feeling the echoes of his son silhouetted in the bedroom of his old house, John knew The Ripper was feeding the distraction into his memories. Rather than follow the dark tendrils back into his own mind, John forced his attention to be fixed in the here and now of the moment. Casting aside the floating letters of the chalk passage that had displayed the prophecy in plain sight for decades, John waited until the room was empty save for the collection of people around the now empty coffin.

'You may leave us.' The Ripper hissed at Qamar and Diana. 'This is a fight of *im*mortals.

'We should be here, in case...' The Ripper ended Qamar's words with a stern glare.

'In case I fail?' The Riper hissed. 'What would a *man* do in such circumstances? This is not a fight for you.'

'We shall watch from the platform.' Taking his leave, Qamar motioned for Diana and Kimberley's escort to follow him out of the chamber.

'You're in for a good show.' John offered Kimberley as she was dragged away. 'One for the ages.'

'Enough words.' The Ripper barked, and attacked.

Pulling his upper body back, John was forced off balance as the Liston blade sliced through the air where his head had been a split second before. Knowing this was his original foe, John knew this fight would be far more challenging than the on in the Zassuru crypt. Rotating himself away, John bounded back towards the far wall with The Ripper on his heels behind him. Reaching the wall, John pressed his foot against the uneven stone and used it as leverage to launch himself up and over The Ripper. Landing behind his opponent, John moved strike strike as a solid elbow crashed into his chest sending him flying back across the room.

Crashing to the floor, John skidded along the polished stone until his back slammed into the corner of the empty coffin. Absorbing the impact, the coffin fell from its supports and dropped to the ground. Hearing the sound of cracking stone, the coffin snapped into two distinct pieces as John used the edge to stand himself up.

'There will be no respite in an eternity of darkness.' The Ripper spat as he charged towards John. 'I will not offer you a tortured banishment, I will destroy you.'

Their fight dominated every inch of the vast cavernous chamber. Pivoting around the broken coffin, John pushed The Ripper back sending shards of shattered stone flying in all direction as the hulking demon lost his footing. Relentless in their battle, neither could find advantage overt the other. Each attack and parry was met with another, until John realised their minds were still connected.

Whatever world of memory The Ripper had forced him into, be them his own or The Ripper's, it soon became clear their connection was still open. Feeling himself predicting each movement of The Ripper, John knew the other creature could sense the same. Offering a feigned attack, John slammed the escrima stick into The Ripper's throat, propelling him back and giving himself enough time to try and break free of their connection.

'If we fight like this, there will never be a victor.' John gasped as he backed around the coffin. 'While ever we are connected, this will be an unending dance of devils.'

As the words left his lips, John knew he had pushed too far. Despite his resistance, the world around him dimmed a little, and John watched as the room was suddenly occupied with the sea of robed disciples around him once again. Fighting to shake away the vision he knew was not real, the figures remained unmoving around him. Stalking to the nearest. John ripped the hood back and recoiled at the face that looked back at him. Although adult in size and stature, the exposed face from beneath the hood was that of his son.

'Why did you leave us?' His son's voice echoed around the room as John backed into another of the robed figures. 'Didn't you love me?'

John was awash with panic as he ripped back another hood to find his son's face once again looking at him. Despite knowing it was not real, seeing the hurt and pain in his son's face sent emotions swirling in his head. Moving through the rows of figures, John set about pulling the hoods back and watched as every face was that of his young son.

'This isn't you.' John hollered as he pushed away the nearest figure.

Distracted by the sea of faces that all moved in unison, following his every panicked move, The Ripper's attack came completely by surprise. Dragging the Moon Blade across John's chest, he felt the burning fire of the cursed blade tore through his skin. Recoiling back, John could see no sign of The Ripper as the vast chamber slowly filled with rolling mist.

'There's nothing for you in this world.' The Ripper taunted as he struck again, this time tracing the blade across John's shoulder blades.

Thrashing out blindly, his weapons failed to find their mark, leaving only a trail in the rolling mist that surrounded him.

'Fight me fairly.' John growled as he caught sight of a shadowy figure in the mist.

Moving towards him, John dropped low and struck as the silhouette appeared in front of him. Feeling the escrima sticks connect, John yelled as he lifted his opponent into the air and slammed him down onto the solid ground. Hoping to see The Ripper beneath him, John growled as he saw his son's face looking up at him. Bloodied and bruised John recoiled in disgust as the tears flowed from his son's eyes.

'I'm sorry.' John stammered as he backed away.

Hearing The Ripper's attack at the last minute, John turned around and avoided the Moon Blade that has been aimed at the back of his head. Feeling the blade bite across his upper arm, he was grateful for his heightened senses as he once again watched The Ripper disappear into the mist.

'Where would the fun be, if I fought fair?'

Looking to the inverted domed ceiling, John saw the mist had not filled the room and quickly launched himself up onto the roof. Anchoring himself to the roof, John could now see The Ripper moving among the sea of robed figures. Hunting from above, John was certain The Ripper was unaware of his move and stayed low as he staled his opponent from above.

Timing his attack, John waited until The Ripper moved beneath him and dropped down to intercept his movements. Timed to perfection, John dropped from the roof with both his weapons held out for an attack. His feet never touched the floor, as The Ripper thrust out the Liston Knife and buried it to the hilt in John's right shoulder. His descent was abruptly stopped as John hung in the air, pinned against the jagged blade. Glaring down at The Ripper, John fought to break free of the blade that now protruded out of his back.

'No escaping your own mind.' The Ripper taunted as it twisted the knife in his shoulder. 'The strongest prison is the one of your own making.'

Out of desperation, John hammered his fists down on The Ripper who accepted each blow without flinching. Knowing he was losing, fighting not to allow the panic to set in, John rotated the escrima stick in his hand and drove it down onto The Ripper's muscular shoulder. Feeling his opponent's grip weaken, John kicked out with both legs and lifted himself off the jagged knife, allowing him to drop like a stone to the floor. Aware it would be a short-lived reprieve, John rolled away and felt hands grasping at him as the robed disciples tried to wrestle him to the ground.

Knowing they were only memories, taunting depictions of a forgotten life and nothing more, John thrashed to break free.

'This isn't my world.' John screamed in anger. 'This is nothing more than your world and your games.'

As he spoke, everything around him froze in place. The only movement came from The Ripper who stalked among the rigid figures and John watched his movement like a hawk. Unwilling to let The Ripper move out of his attention, the world once again faded around him until the chamber had taken on its more familiar appearance again. Seeing the shattered coffin to his side, John watched as The Ripper hovered in the darker shadows of the room, beneath the raised platform where Diana, Qamar, Kimberley and her escort were now standing.

'It seems your time in her hospital has dampened your sense.'

As The Ripper spoke, his voice now came from behind him as John turned to locate the source. Much to his surprise, The Ripper was now stood a short distance away, behind where he had been a second before. Frustrated by his lack of awareness, John knew his senses and powers were being distracted by the lingering connection with The Ripper. Hitting his own head in frustration, John saw the world glitching before him. Seeing the distorted views of multiple worlds, John hit his head harder and caught sight of The Ripper as he attacked again.

Lunging forward, John saw the shimmer of the golden blade as The Ripper dragged it up towards his torso. Already on the back foot, John dropped to the left side and moved to catch The Ripper's powerful arm as it attacked. Catching the demon's wrist, John used the momentum of the attack to drag The Ripper around and send the Moon Blade clattering to the floor. Unable to follow the weapon's path, John set about wrapping his body around the muscular arm and pulling with all his strength to break the bone. Hearing the satisfying *crunch*, John released his grip and backed away from the cowering Ripper, now nursing his broken arm.

Unbeknown to John, there was no Ripper in front of him. He had done nothing more than fight with a figment of his own imagination. The now cowering Ripper was not real and while a look of pride and satisfaction appeared on his face beneath the mask, it promptly disappeared as The Ripper in front of him disintegrated into a pile of smouldering ash.

'You have lost your way.' The Ripper oozed, grinning at the genuine look of surprise on John's face. 'You have forgotten yourself as Death's Hand. You are nothing more than a lost soul, absent from either world of life or death.'

without warning, The Ripper launched himself at John..

19

THE SACRIFICE

From their vantage point, none of the observers could make sense of the fight between the two of them. The speed and manner of their fight was impossible to track as they each used their environment to their advantage. Propelling up, over, around and through, John's movements were significantly slower than The Ripper's. Denying any potential end to the furious fight, John used his escrima sticks to keep The Ripper at bay more often than driving in attacks.

As John moved to disarm the Moon Blade from The Ripper's grasp, he once again felt a sting of pain as the blade bit into his forearm. Recoiling from the attack, John lost his footing as The Ripper slammed his elbow down onto his neck. Pounded into the ground, John's head span with the force of the blow and he fought with desperation to keep his senses from shutting down. Ducking beneath the protection of his arms, a second elbow smashed into his temple and provided enough distraction to allow The Ripper to slam his fist into John's face.

Hearing bones give way beneath the blow, John was grateful he could not feel the accompanying pain. Lifted from the floor by the power of the attack, John had no time to react as The Ripper raised the Moon Blade up and drove the hooked blade down onto the top of his head. Flinching from the attack, John succeeded, more by luck than skill, to avoid the blade cleaving his head in two and screamed in pain as the blade sank into his collar.

'You are mine.' The Ripper grunted through gritted teeth as he pulled his whole weight down on the blade.

Knees buckling under the immense weight and strength of The Ripper, John dropped to the ground. Fighting against the vice-like grip, John fought to pull the blade free from his shoulder with no success. Head swimming with the burning pain that coursed through him, John hammered his right arm into The Ripper's chest and head but felt no give in the blade. Snatching the plague doctor mask form his face, John found himself nose-to-nose with The Ripper.

'After everything, you are nothing more than a man.' The Ripper snarled.

Seeing his reflection in The Ripper's burning eyes, John fought to break free. Feeling no give, he knew he was done for unless he could find a way to break free.

'At least I remember where I came from.' John coughed, every word bringing with it a fresh wave of pain through his body.

'You're not the only one.' The Ripper smirked as he leaned closer, allowing him to speak with John almost intimately. 'You were born out of desperation, a desperate act by a powerless creature. I was born from power and strength.'

'You were made in the depths of hell.'

'I need no soul of my own to become what I am.'

'No, you feed on others to stay alive.' John coughed. 'You're nothing more than a cancer.'

'Call it what you will, but when I assume my mantle on the throne you delivered to me, I will be free to release my army on this world.'

'To what end?'

'There will be no end.'

Sensing movement in his peripheral vision, John turned to look towards the shattered coffin as the pieces of stone shuddered on the ground. Watching on in disbelief, John saw the pieces lift form the ground and rotate in the air. Joined by every piece of the shattered coffin, John could only watch as the pieces reformed themselves into the shape of a curious throne. The very place that John had confined The Ripper all those years ago, was now the means to The Ripper's ascension if he failed.

As the floating chair settled in the centre of the chamber, John reached to his boot and removed a short dagger. Keeping The Ripper's attention from his movements, John timed his attack as The Ripper started speaking again. The moment he returned his attention to John, he attacked. Thrusting the dagger up through the air, John's attack found its mark as the dagger sank to the hilt between The Ripper's ribs. Recoiling from the attack, The Ripper staggered backwards, ripping the Moon

Blade from John's shoulder and neck. Favouring his injured neck, John staggered back and watched as The Ripper ripped the dagger free from his side and dropped it to the ground.

'Is that how desperate you are?' The Ripper grumbled as he glared at John. 'A mortal dagger cannot hurt me.'

Knowing he was fast running out of moves, John looked around the room for help. Seeing Kimberley's terrified expression, he was about to say something when The Ripper moved. To the observers, The Ripper's attack was too fast to comprehend.

To John it happened in slow motion.

Still holding the Moon Blade, The Ripper surged forward and John had nowhere to move. Preparing himself for the attack, John saw the glint of the blade as The Ripper dragged the weapon low to the ground before bringing it up towards John's torso.

John felt nothing as the Moon Blade bit into his right thigh and dragged diagonally across his abdomen and chest. Finishing the attack with a defiant war cry, John struggled to comprehend what had happened before his knees buckled beneath him. Raising both hands to the jagged wound, he heard Kimberley's scream of terror but kept his attention fixed on The Ripper. For the first time in decades, John felt blood on his fingers and looked down to see his hands thick with his own blood.

'How?' John croaked as The Ripper stalked over to him.

'The Moon Blade gives, before it takes.' The Ripper smirked as he admired the ornate weapon. 'And with it, the prophecy is complete.'

Hooking the blade on his belt, The Ripper took hold of John's collar and lifted him into the air. As a sensation of weakness consumed him, John could do nothing to fight back.

'Leave him.' Kimberley screamed but fell silent with a solid blow from her escort.

'I'll be fine.' John offered a feigned smile as he struggled to turn his head to look up at her. 'I've been in worse situations than this.'

'Take your last look at your life.' The Ripper hissed in his ear.

John knew he was done. Judging by the look on Kimberley's face, she knew it too. Rather than plea or offer anything to give The Ripper pleasure in his defeat, all he did was close his eyes.

Vision blurred by the tears in her eyes, Kimberley watched as The Ripper took hold of John's shoulders and violently pulled them apart. Had she not been aware of the world she had now been exposed to, the sight of John being torn in half would have seemed impossible.

There was no blood to accompany the violent motion. Like a snake shedding its skin, Kimberley watched as John's long dead body slumped to the ground at The Ripper's feet. In a state of decay, there was no life in the pile of tattered clothes and bones. As for John's existence as The Raven, the torn exterior disintegrated in The Ripper's hands until there was nothing left but the lifeless corpse on the ground.

'It is done.' Qamar yelled in excitement. 'The prophecy is fulfilled and you are victorious.'

Kimberley's attention was fixed on John's corpse and she paid no attention to the delighted exchanges between Qamar and Diana. Allowing the tears to roll down her cheeks, it was a curious feeling and one she could not explain. Her emotions were a mix of frustration that John appeared to have given up mixed with grief at her loss and fear of what was to come. Feeling herself released from her escort's grip, Kimberley shrugged herself free and sprinted down the steps leading back down to the main chamber floor.

'Let her go." Diana's voice declared behind her, but she paid the woman no attention.

Dropping to her knees, Kimberley rolled over the decayed corpse and lifted John's body onto her lap. What tethers of flesh were left on the mottled skull bore no resemblance to the face she knew. Empty eyesockets looked up at her as she allowed her tears to fall onto the discoloured bone. Looking at the discoloured fabric, she realised John was dressed in the same uniform he had been wearing the night of his murder. Removing the silver crest from the collar of his tunic, she held it in her clenched fist as the chamber started to fill with the robed disciples retaking their place before the platform.

'You've had enough time to say goodbye.' Diana hushed in Kimberley's ear. 'You don't need to be part of this.'

'Go to hell.' Kimberley spat and pulled herself away from Diana's grasp.

'Hell is coming here.' Diana hushed. 'And I would not see you consumed by it.'

Pulling Kimberley away from John's corpse, his body slumped to the ground as Diana dragged her back to the stone steps leading to the platform above the chamber. Offering minimal resistance, Kimberley turned her back on John's remains as it disappeared behind the reforming rows of robed figures. Reaching the bottom of the steps, she heard The Ripper addressing the disciples and turned to listen to his victorious declaration as the followers filed back into the crypt.

'For decades I have waited for this moment.' The Ripper scanned the sea of shadowed hoods. 'Your devotion, and the guidance of your leader, has brought this moment of victory.'

'You defeated The Raven,' Qamar interjected. 'You prevailed and fulfilled the prophecy.'

'You honour me with your devotion. But the journey has only just begun.' The Ripper moved to the curiously constructed stone chair in the centre of the chamber. 'By assuming my position on the throne, the barriers to Sub Terra will be mine to control and we will no longer be prisoners to an archaic system.'

Admiring the throne, The Ripper took a moment to drink in its curious design.

'The people are amassed above us,' a voice declared from the gathered disciples. 'They litter the streets, ready to become the vessels to your will.'

'Everything has led to this moment.' Diana continued as she left Kimberley unattended at the bottom of the stairs and moved up to join Qamar.

'No longer will my kind be bound by the Rule Of One.' The Ripper's tone changed, his voice more passionate. 'Too long have wee been confined and imprisoned, creatures of shadow and death. That ends tonight.'

The room was filled with cheers.

'I have honoured every caveat, broken no promise and now claim my rightful place as Guardian Of The Gates.' Turning around, The Ripper moved to sit on the throne. 'The Dark Angel made me in her image. A warrior. A survivor. An idol.'

As The Ripper sat on the throne, the chamber was bathed in a blinding light. Turning from the light, Kimberley glimpsed Diana as she stalked onto the platform, holding John's discarded dagger behind her back before the light was too bright to keep her eyes open.

'LET THE GATES BE OPEN.' The Ripper announced, and in response, the room shook.

20

IT IS DONE

'This isn't how I expected it to end.' John coughed as he lay on the dusty floor staring up at the vaulted ceiling. 'Where am I?'

'You're with me now.' Azrael replied as he materialised over John.

'I failed, didn't I?' John huffed as he accepted Azrael's hand and allowed himself to be lifted from the floor.

'You're here because I misjudged you.' Azrael wasn't angry, John could hear the disappointment in his voice which hurt even more. 'I thought you could be my hand, but I asked too much of you.'

'I'm not done.' John protested as he fell into step behind Azrael. 'I can go back, I can finish what I started.'

'You can't.' Azrael replied as he pushed open an ornate set of wooden doors.

Bathed in bright sunshine, it took a moment for John's eyes to adjust to the harsh sunlight. Looking through the open door, the sight before him was like nothing he had seen before. A city stretched out into the distance, all polished marble and stone that flowed towards an enormous dome in the city's centre.

'Is this heaven?' John gasped as he stepped through the door and onto a wide balcony overlooking the impressive city.

'This is somewhere else, a place between what you term heaven and hell.' Azrael did not join John on the balcony's edge, instead he headed to another set of ornate doors further along the balcony. 'We aren't staying.'

Taking a moment to drink in the impressive beauty of the curious city, John eventually turned his attention to Azrael who now held the other doors open. Knowing he had no choice but to follow, he moved across the balcony and joined Azrael.

'So, where are you taking me?'

'To the Knight's Bridge.' Azrael's tone was far more serious as he stepped through the new set of doors. 'Follow me.'

The moment Azrael crossed the threshold, he disappeared, leaving John alone on the polished balcony. Taking another look at the magnificent city and shimmering dome in the bright sunlight, John turned his attention to the door and followed Azrael. Feeling a curious tug in his navel, John was ripped from the doorway and transported through a flurry of lights and motion. Losing all sense of direction, John's body was overcome with a sensation of nausea and clamped his eyes shut in an attempt to stop himself from being sick.

Crashing to the ground, John tumbled head over foot and came to rest in a shallow stream of tumbling water. Dizzy and disorientated, John lay back in the water and allowed his vision to stop spinning as he tried to make sense of where he was. Unlike the city of marble, all he could see at first was a heavy clouded sky and the branches of a cherry tree in blossom. Seeing the pink blossom swaying in the gentle breeze, John felt relief as the world slowly stopped spinning.

'What is this place?' John quizzed as he sat up in the rolling stream. 'It's beautiful.'

Sensing movement, John looked around and realised he was now in some sort of Japanese water garden. The landscape stretched as far as he could see and was a mix of meandering streams, ornate bridges and cherry trees in blossom. Figures moved along the footpaths and bridges but nobody was near him, except for Azrael.'

'This isn't what it seems.' There was a sadness in his voice as he spoke. 'This is where you now belong.'

'Why do I get the feeling it's not as peaceful as it seems.' John clambered up the banks of the stream and joined Azrael on the wooden bridge.

'I'm sorry it has come to this.'

'I thought you took people to their afterlife, to heaven or hell?'

'Those destined for ascent or descent don't need my protection.' Azrael sighed as he leant on the bridge and looked over the landscape. 'My role is to gather those whose lives are undecided, whose fate is not clear and present them to the Council in Altum.'

'Is that the place we were at before?' Azrael answered only with a saddened nod as he removed his hood. 'Is my fate decided then, is this my version of heaven?'

Watching the skin take shape covering the exposed skull, the last thing to appear were Azrael's melancholy eyes. Seeing the expression, John felt a sense of dread as he back away from his robed companion and scanned the figures in the distance once again.

Seeing one figure move closer, John could see it was a medieval knight in a state of decomposed decay. Tattered flesh and battered armour, the silent warrior stalked across the nearby bridge, paying no attention to Azrael or John. Disturbed by the sight of the knight, John watched the figure follow the path before bringing his attention back to Azrael.

'This is a place between all things. It will be your resting place, for eternity.'

'What?'

John was on Azrael in a heartbeat. Gripping the collar of Azrael's robes, he pressed the other man hard against the side of the bridge. Glaring into the lifeless eyes of Death, John saw his reflection in Azrael's eyes. Overcome with anger, John fought to make sense of what was happening. After all he had done for Azrael, despite his mistakes, it had always been on the belief he would find an end some day, and end that would reconcile him with his family. As he stared at his own reflection, it dawned on John that he had never asked about his fate when his duty was done.

'I am so sorry.' Azrael began as John released his grip and backed away. 'You were never meant for death when The Ripper took you. This was the only way to ensure you would not be lost into the afterlife.'

'Lost?'

'The souls The Ripper feeds on remain in a place even I cannot go. Unfinished and incomplete, their lives are nothing more than shadows and their deaths are plagued by the dishonour of what he has done to them.'

'Where do they go?'

'Nowhere.' Azrael sighed as he watched John struggling to make sense of what was being said. 'They are the ghosts of your world, empty spirits with no purpose or finality, haunting the lives that were wrongfully taken from them.'

'I don't want that.'

'Which is why you are here.'

'Is this any better?' John looked across at the decaying knight who had taken a seat leaning against a tree trunk, watching them from a distance. 'Is this peaceful? They don't look at peace.'

'It's better than being driven mad by the life you lost.'

'This isn't fair.'

'Nothing is fair in death,' Azrael offered as he moved to stand in front of John. 'For what it's worth, I had hoped when the time came to come here, you would know everything.'

'That would help if you hadn't abandoned me.'

'This again?' Azrael fought not to raise his voice in the tranquillity of Knight's Bridge. 'My purpose was not to interfere, perhaps to nudge you in the right direction, but the Nuthall severed all of that.'

'I did what I thought was best.'

'As did I.'

They were clearly at an impasse, neither man wanting to acknowledge that this was the end. Despite his composure, John could see the regret in Azrael's face and choose to look away. Allowing his gaze to settle on the decaying medieval knight, he watched as the figure beckoned for him to join him. Waving its boned fingers, John felt Azrael's presence behind him.

'You deserve more than this, a better end than this place.' Azrael hushed. 'But I cannot defy the covenants that guide my role a Death.'

'It's a shame the other side don't see it the same way.'

'That is what differentiates us from evil.' Azrael placed his hand on John's shoulder. 'If we lower our standards to their level, we become the very thing we swore to protect humanity from. I cannot defy my promises, and for that reason, this will be your home.'

'Is this it then?' John refused to look at Azrael. 'After everything, you'll leave me here to become the same as him?'

Admiring the familiarity of his work uniform, John realised he would be nothing more than another dead police constable in this place. Although he looked across at the knight, he expected there would be many a warrior or protector wandering among the blossoming trees. Despite himself, he could not deny the peacefulness that hung in the air as the trees swayed lazily in the gentle breeze.

'I must return,' Azrael chose his next words with care. 'The events with the Society have put our balance in jeopardy. I must work to remedy what has happened.'

'I'm sorry I wasn't better.' John confessed as he pulled away from Azrael's grasp. 'You should have chosen someone else.'

Unable to find the right words, Azrael could only watch as John descended the bridge and followed the pebbled path towards the beckoning knight. Feeling a heavy sense of melancholy, Azrael waited for John to join the knight before taking his leave. As the two strangers made their introductions, Azrael disappeared from the Knight's Bridge.

'Welcome home, brother.' The knight declared as he rose to his feet. 'You will have many questions, I expect.'

'You could say that.' John replied as he cast a glance back at the now empty bridge. 'I'm not sure what happens next.'

'Shall we take a walk, and I will explain what this place is and why you are here.'

Accepting the invitation, John admired the curious knight's decaying face. In any other circumstance, John would have been repulsed by the vision of the partially exposed bone and discoloured flesh that clung to the man's cheeks and chin. Despite the rotting flesh, the knight's eyes were bright and filled with the life that his body no longer showed. Falling into step beside the labouring knight, John listened to everything the ancient man had to tell him as they explored the never-ending landscape of the Knight's Bridge.

Despite his own lingering disappointment in defeat, the worries for the world he had left behind soon felt like a distant memory. Hanging on every word the knight spoke, John's mind soon released its grip on the tendrils of disappointment and regret he felt. As the day progressed and the never-moving sun occasionally broke through the rolling clouds, John allowed himself to be touched and swallowed by the peaceful tranquility of his surroundings.

The end had finally come, and while it was not the one he had hoped for, John could not deny he finally felt at peace. Whatever happened next in London was of no concern to him. His future was here, and if he had learned on thing, his connection to the past was something he would have to give up.

'I'm here now,' John muttered under his breath as the knight guided him onto another wooden bridge overlooking an impressive waterfall. 'I may not be with you, but I'm no longer lost. I miss you.'

It may have been in his imagination, but as John admired the tumbling water cascading over the jagged rocks, he was sure he heard the laughter of his son and his wife's voice calling in the distance.

He was done.

A forgotten sentinel, recruited by Death, given his peace.

—— • ——

EPISODE

VI

RESURRECTION

21

— · —

CONDUITS AND LINES

The streets were alive with people, all unaware of what was happening beneath their feet. Oblivious to the dark and dangerous rituals in the secret underground structures, the chatter of voices was high-spirited. In the time since John and Kimberley had been carted through the grounds and into the concealed entrance, the streets had been filled with stalls and vendors. Lights flashed and music blared from speakers mounted to the lampposts, drowning out any sign that the gathered crowds were in the heart of London.

With cars diverted from the closed street, the road was filled with revellers of all ages. Although the crowds were mostly made up of younger souls, the crowd itself was rich and diverse. Despite the splattering of rain, nobody seemed to care as groups danced and chatted in small huddles, covering every inch of the space reserved for the Blood Moon Celebrations.

Ever under the watchful eyes of the Full Moon Society, the pair of robed figures that watched from the rooftop on the opposite of New Inn Street observed the crowds. Shrouded in the shadows of the rooftop, it was doubtful the crowds of people has paid them any notice from the streets below.

'Do you think they will succeed?' The robed woman quizzed as she moved to join her companion leant against the crumbling rooftop edge.

'Don't let anyone hear you asking that.' The man snapped. 'You'll be ousted if they think you're losing faith.'

'It's not that I'm losing faith, far from it, it's just that it all sounds so impossible.'

'You know the prophecy, as we all do. We've never been so close.'

'I know.' Her voice trailed off as the music skipped below.

Peering over the ledge, neither of them saw anything different about the street and nobody appeared to have noticed the sudden skip in the beat. Resting her elbows on the crumbling stone, the young woman removed her hood and looked down at the crowds below. Bathed in the eerie glow of a flickering light, her eyes appeared cold and lifeless, and yet she was not what anyone would have expected from a Society member. Instead of wise and serious beyond her years, the woman was only in her early twenties and sported a rose tattoo down the side of her neck. Anywhere else, dressed in any other way, she could easily have been mistaken for one of the revellers below.

'When will we know if they have succeeded?' She pressed as a trio of rowdy young men barreled into a group and an argument broke out between them.

'Beyond the words of the prophecy, I don't think anyone knows what will happen.' The man sighed as he watched the fight escalating. 'But I am, certain there will be no doubt when it does.'

'Look!' Pushing away from the wall, the young woman's attention was drawn to a curious mist that had begun billowing from the open grates and manholes scattered around the street.

At first she had dismissed the smoke as some party effect from some unseen machine beneath the array of stalls, but the way it moved seemed wrong. Feeling the breeze on her face, she soon realised the smoke was flowing against the wind. As it moved among the crowds, enveloping their legs and feet, she could see it had an eerie red hue to the rolling mist.

'What is that?'

'Maybe it's the sign?'

As if to answer their questions, the mist suddenly exploded skyward. Reacting on instinct, both of them lurched back as the fountain of mist reached its peak level with the rooftop. Shrouding the street from the rest of the world, the mist travelled the length of the street before creating a physical wall between New Inn Street and the surrounding roads. Despite its sinister appearance, the crowd simply cheered, seemingly believing it to be some fanciful display to charge the crowd's excitement. Seeing the cascade of crimson cloud climb into the air, all eyes watched with dumbfound excitement as the clouds soon spread above the street, shrouding everything in a hazy blood-red sheen.

'They must think it's something to do with the party.' The woman gasped as she watched the mysterious mist billowing out from its source.

'Fools.' The man replied as he admired the clouds that hovered just the other side of the rooftop edge. 'It's amazing.'

There was something about the way the mist moved, almost serpentine, as if something moved beneath the turbulent mist.

'What do you think it is?' The woman hushed as she moved closer to peer into the shadows of the clouds.

As close as she was, she could feel the electricity on her skin as the hair on her arms stood on end. Pressing her face closer to the crimson mist, she saw the shadows moving within. Awash with curiosity, she moved closer to the swirling clouds until she could feel the tangible chill as it hovered millimeters from her skin.

'Don't do that.' Her companion barked, but it was pointless. Something had been ignited inside her brain and all she could hear were the soft whispers that invited her closer. Drowning out the warning of her companion, she allowed her nose to push through the thin veneer of mist, followed by her face. Pushing through, she could feel the wisps of mist across her face, like fingers dancing over her skin. Keeping her eyes open, she did not know what to expect as the red mist enveloped her head and muted out any view other than the moving shadows somewhere within the clouds.

At last her face broke through the other side and the view that greeted her sent an icy shiver down her spine. The view of the street was completely different. The crowds were no longer consumed by the joy of their party. Instead, from her vantage point above, the crowds were thrashing wildly on the ground as if if their bodies no longer did as they were told. As the bodies lay writhing on the ground, the young woman realised she was no longer stood on the rooftop and was somehow floating in the air above the crowds. Beyond all realm of possibility, she was somehow flying in the air above the street with nothing beneath her feet.

'You taste different.' A sinister voice hissed from the rolling clouds in front of her. 'You don't feel as weak as them.'

'What's happening?' The woman stammered as she fought to turn around and return to the safety of the rooftop.

'You see the freedom your prophecy has allowed?' The voice was hushed and tainted with a London twang.

'All I see are panicked people.' The young woman protested as she tried to claw her way back to the rooftop.

'Then let me show you.'

As the words were uttered, her view of the ground below changed. Where she had seen nothing but a see of twisting and contorting bodies, she now saw a sea of demons fighting to pin their victims to the ground. The flailing and panic was in fact their attempts to break free from the surge of demonic creatures that yearned to feed from them.

'I'm not part of this.' The woman shrieked as she watched a shadowy spectre climb into a young man it had pinned to the road.

'You're here now.' The voice sounded close but she could see nothing. 'You're mine now. There is no going back.'

With a flash of lightning, the woman screamed as The Ripper apparated in the air in front of her. Taking in his appearance, the panic sent her heart racing in her chest. His charred skin, ghoulish eyes and floating jacket added to the fear that boiled inside her. Powerless to resist his approach, she felt her arms pinned to her side as The Ripper simply reached out towards her chest.

'Please.' The woman sobbed as his gloved hand touched her solar plexus. 'I don't want to die.'

'This isn't death,' The Ripper smirked. 'Death is not coming for you. I am.'

Surging forward, the young woman felt nothing as The Ripper drove its clawed hand through flesh and bone, taking hold of her still beating heart. Ripping it from her chest, the woman's lifeless body dropped to he ground and landed in an awkward pile among the sea of people. As the Ripper devoured the woman's heart, he lowered himself from his vantage point and grinned as the demons infecting the partygoers shuffled away, giving him space to land. Ignoring the terrified humans that littered the road, The Ripper kept his attention only on the creatures from his own world.

'My brothers and sisters of Sub Terra.' The Ripper announced dramatically as he wiped the blood from his lips. 'We are at last free from the confines of our imprisonment. An unfair imprisonment that has eroded the might of our great people.'

'Lies and corruption.' One demon sang from gathered attentive faces.

These demons were different than anything before, unlike the Imps and Revenants, they lacked features and stood merely shadows. Human in size, shape and stature, the only tell-tale sign of human features were the shimmering green eyes and toothless mouths that chattered silently. Admiring he sea of spectral figures, The Ripper swelled with pride as he lifted the woman's corpse from the ground. Allowing the oversized robe to slip from her shoulders, he took a moment to admire his own reflection in the dead woman's eyes.

Seeing himself framed by the familiar colours of his origins, all fear of what could have passed were gone. Known only to The Ripper, his victory over the Raven had almost come as a surprise. Knowing both their connections to the afterlife was weakened, he had been surprised to deliver to the final blow. Casting aside the embarrassment his fear had created in him, The Ripper disregarded the dead woman's body and returned his attention to his audience.

'Where you have been denied existence and forced to live as nothing more than echoes of what was. I give you now the means to return. Claim these fetid beings as your own. Consume them, become them and once again the might of Sub Terra, of their HELL shall rise.'

The spectral demons erupted into a chorus of excitement. Walking back towards the old school building, The Ripper beamed with pride as the creatures parted to make way for him. Leaving the street behind, The Ripper heard the panicked screams of the demon's victims as they set about consuming their bodies from the inside. To his side, he watched as one demon set about climbing into the open mouth of a middle-aged man frozen in mid-scream.

To anyone but The Ripper, the grotesque creature twisting and contorting itself into the man's body would have been an unsettling sight. To The Ripper, it was the inevitable way of things. Without a human host, the Demonites could only exist in the living realm for a limited time. Where The Ripper could survive on his exposures to human life, the Demonites required a full human host to survive. Feeling a surge of sympathy for them, The Ripper turned his back on the sea of bodies and returned into the secret subterranean complex beneath the street.

Having left the room the moment he had sat on the throne, The Ripper could not help but swell with pride as he prepared to present himself before the Society. After all they had done, the oaths honoured and rituals performed, he now stood as the guardian of the gates. Steeling himself for a rapturous reception, The Ripper pushed open the doors and felt his heart sink at the sheer panic that filled the room.

Scanning the scattering crowds, his attention fell to the raised platform where Qamar lay, clutching at the dagger that now protruded from his stomach.

Before he could speak, The Ripper sensed the attack and moved just in time to another Tarnished Blade cleaving his head in two. Turning his attention to the would-be assassin, it took a moment to register the fact it was not Kimberley or even The Raven who wielded the sword.

It was the last person he had expected to see.

22

A LIFE OF CHANCES

J ohn sat alone beneath the cherry blossom tree, admiring the view across the expanse of the Knight's Bridge garden. Hearing the tumbling water in the stream at his feet, there was something serene about where he found himself. Having taken his leave from the company of the nameless knight, he had found a place to sit and ponder what was to come.

It was impossible to understand the passage of time. The shimmering sun that peeked between the clouds did not appear to have moved since he had arrived. To John, it felt as if he had been banished to a world that would offer no end or finality. Resting his head back against the smooth trunk of the tree he looked at the fluttering blossom that tumbled from the tree, unsettled by the gentle breeze. Reaching out his hand, John caught a handful of the petals in his hand and revelled in the fact he could at last *feel* something.

Where his life beyond the grave had severed his connection to mortal feelings, there was no denying the tender tickle of the blossom against his palm. Admiring the soft pink petal, he watched as it promptly withered and decayed in his hand. As the petals disintegrated to ash, he brushed the debris from his hand and returned his attention to the stream.

'You'll soon find yourself like those petals.' A softer voice offered from the bridge behind him. 'That is the curse of this place.'

'So I'm destined to sit and watch myself wither?' John huffed, refusing to turn his head to look at the new arrival. 'What a reward for all I've done.'

'You expect reward?' The soft voice quizzed. 'What did you do to deserve such a prize?'

'I gave everything.'

'You were given everything. You gave very little in return.'

Frustrated by the response, John launched up from the tree and turned to face the bridge. Somewhat taken aback by the diminutive figure that stood looking at him, it was not what he had expected. Having thought the voice belonged to the knight who had welcomed him to the Knight's bridge, he now looked at a weathered old man he did not recognise. Unlike the other inhabitants, this man was not decayed, instead he looked just to be an old man nearing the end of a long life. Resting on a crooked cane, there was something familiar about the old man's features, but John could not put his finger on it.

'Who are you?'

'Maybe I'm your conscience?' The old man replied with a playful smile. 'Or maybe I'm just the poor orphan who has spent a lifetime watching you.'

'Say what you need to and then leave me alone.'

'To what end?' the old man asked as he made his way down the slope bridge, careful to keep his balance. 'Are you going to once again withdraw into yourself and allow your mind to hibernate as you did in the hospital?'

'You don't know what you're talking about!' John snapped as the old man reached the grass and turned to face him.

'I know the man you were before, and this is not him.' The old man remained on the path's edge and put all his weight on the crooked cane. 'You've become an empty shell, nothing more than an echo of the man you once were.'

'What am I supposed to do? This is my fate now.' The frustration was hard to control as John defended himself against the words of the weathered man. 'It's not like I asked to be here.'

'Didn't you?'

'How dare you?' John was on the old man in two strides and towered over him. 'Who are you to say that, you know nothing about me.'

'I know everything about you.' The old man replied, unperturbed by John's towering presence and simply offering him an upward glance at best. 'You committed yourself to this fate when you turned away from the promises you made to Azrael. You became the shell of what you should have been, and so you were never ready to face The Ripper.'

'I thought I had defeated him.'

'You were wrong.' The matter of fact reply angered him.

'No kidding! You don't think I realise that now? I did everything I could, once I knew, to correct that mistake.'

'You would have succeeded, had you been there.' The old man pushed past John and shuffled to the water's edge. 'Why do you think he was so powerful?'

'Because he had the support of the Full Moon Society. They had built everything around that stupid prophecy.'

'It's entirely stupid now, is it?' The old man jibed as he disrupted the flow of water with the tip of his cane. 'If it were so stupid, maybe you wouldn't be standing here.'

'What is your point?'

'Your absence allowed so much to fester and grow. Without the Raven on his perch, watching from the shadows as you were tasked, the darker creatures were allowed to grow in confidence. Your position was never *just* about facing The Ripper.'

'That's not how it was sold to me.'

'It was exactly how it was sold, you simply interpreted it to fit your own narrative and desire for nothing more than revenge.' There was an air of tangible disappointment in the old man's words. 'You were blinded only by your personal desires and forgot your roots.'

'What roots, a dead man lying in an alley? How can I forget that when it haunts me every day?'

Turning around, the old man reached into his pocket and removed a small item he clenched in his shaking fist. Holding out his shaking hand, the old man waited for John to join him and accept the item gripped in his hand. Accepting the theatrical course of their conversation, John placed his open hand beneath the old man's and gasped as a silver badge fell from the old man's hand and into his palm.

'How did you get this?' John gasped, immediately recognising the force crest from his uniform. 'This is mine.'

'Those were your roots, not the day you died, but the days you lived.' The old man explained as he took a step back, leaving John staring in disbelief at the metal badge. 'You once promised your life in service to the people, to protect them from evil and darkness. Your mantle as the Raven was no different, simply a different uniform I suppose.'

'This was buried with me.' John stammered as he brought the badge to his eye line.

'No, it wasn't. It was given to your family.'

'I didn't know.' The emotions that John had suppressed for so long, came flooding back and his knees buckled beneath him.

'Your son held that one thing more dear than anything.' The old man soothed as he moved to John. 'He carried it with him every day, believing you were the hero he could only ever aspire to be. What would he think of you now?'

'I did my best.'

'Could you look him in the eyes and tell him that? Tell him you did your best and this outcome was nothing short of inevitable?'

Lifting John's chin, the old man forced him to look into his eyes as he now stood the same height as John kneeling on the damp grass. Settling his attention on the old man, John searched his features and once again could not shake the fact he felt like he knew the man, that somehow their paths had crossed at some point. Behind the wrinkles and dark rings around his eyes, there was a fire that burned in his eyes.

'Who are you?' John croaked, struggling to find his voice.

'The boy who held onto that as the only memory of a father he never had the honour of knowing.'

John recoiled away from the old man as he suddenly transformed before his eyes. Discarding the cane, John watched as the years disappeared from his face and body until, the familiar face of his son stood on the grass looking at him. Fighting to find the words, John opened and closed his mouth like a dying fish as the words refused to form in his throat.

'I now know you watched me from the shadows.' His son's voice was no longer tainted by his years and once again sounded youthful and vibrant. 'At the time I thought you were lost to me, if I had known you were there it would have been some comfort.'

'I'm sorry.' Was all John could muster.

'You saw me grow but hid when the pain was too much. But I forgive you.' His son retrieved the badge from John's hand. 'Did you do your best?'

'I thought I had.'

'That's not an answer.' His son corrected. 'Did you do your best, did you honour your oath or did you hide when the path was no longer the one you believed it was?'

'I hid.' John confessed, his shoulders dropping with the weight of his confession.

'You missed my daughter's birth and the family that followed her. Perhaps you would have known Kimberley's importance, but you wouldn't have needed to know if you had been true to the Raven.'

'I'm sorry.'

'You would have seen the poisonous whispers of the Dark Angel that manipulated the Full Moon Society for her own gain and perhaps your paths would never have crossed.'

'Please, this is torture.' John pleaded. 'You stand there highlighting my mistakes and the heavy cost, knowing there is nothing I can do to right those wrongs.'

'Would you though, if you could?'

'Of course.' John snapped. 'Why would I sit here and do nothing?'

'You did before.' His son's words hit like a brick.

'That was, that was different. I didn't know.'

'You chose not to know.'

'But Azrael never explained it to me. He could have corrected my course.'

'It was not for him to do that.' His son sighed. 'Azrael honours the ways of old, limiting his interference in matters of the living. The same cannot be said for the Dark Angel Amber.'

'And that is why I can offer you this.'

John turned at the arrival of an all too familiar voice. Much to his surprise, Azrael was once again stood on the arched bridge behind him. Already with his hood removed, John could see his features and the serious expression on Azrael's face. Looking to his hand, John saw the plague doctor mask gripped in Azraels' gloved hand. Jumping to his feet, John moved stand in the water beneath the bridge, looking up like an expectant child would to their father.

'I thought you said this was my fate?'

'And it was.' Azrael mused as he looked down at John. 'Until I learned of the truth behind the Society's rise and the devious whispers she has planted in the ears of its members.'

'How does that change things?'

'Your banishment to this place was done in honour of covenants made in the drive for balance and order. she has broken that.'

'And their prophecy?'

'Perhaps we are brothers, twins in our own right, and the fight to be had is yet to happen?' Azrael offered John as he dropped the plague doctor mask. 'A prophecy, after all, can always be interpreted.'

Catching the mask, John felt the familiar surge of strength and power the moment the soft leather touched his skin. Admiring the mask, he looked up at Azrael before turning his attention to his son still stood on the banks of the stream.

'I won"t make the same mistakes.' John promised as he moved to place the mask over his face.

'I know dad,' the words stopped him mid-movement. 'You'll make all new ones, but you'll make me proud.'

Eyeing his son, there was nothing more that needed to be said. Offering nothing more than a playful wink, John slipped the mask over his head and waited for the rest of his Raven ensemble to materialise over his body.

'I Ic has your wit,' Azrael offered as he too replaced the hood over his head. 'You should be proud.'

'I am.' Both John and his son replied in unison and it was the last thing John heard before the Knight's Bridge disappeared from view.

23

A LOST SOUL

Correcting the course of the tarnished blade, Diana snarled as she missed her target and fought to keep her balance.

'What is this foolishness?' The Ripper barked as he turned to face Diana. 'It's me. Drop your sword.'

'I know it's you!' Diana barked and thrust the tip of the blade toward him. 'I've waited a lifetime for this.'

Snatching the Moon Blade from his side, The Ripper deflected the second attack and leapt back into the middle of the vast chamber. Amid the sea of terrified and panicked faces, the crowds soon made for the open door as the fighting pair made their way across the room. Moving with impressive skill, Diana was a formidable opponent, and while he longed to understand what was happening, she gave The Ripper no chance to think as the tarnished blade whipped past his face.

Dodging another attack, The Ripper thrust the Moon Blade out at Diana and felt disappointment as the blade was deflected by a downward thrust of the sword in her hand. Dropping back,

Diana rolled over her right shoulder and thrust the pointed tip of her weapon up towards his heart. Blocking the attack, The Ripper took hold of the sword's blade, ignoring the sting of pain and dragged Diana towards him.

'What is this madness?'

Holding her face close to his, The Ripper saw something in Diana's eyes that unnerved him. Glaring into her eyes, he saw a burning fire that felt all too familiar. Pushing her away, he ripped the sword from her grip and tossed it across the room behind him. Staring at her, Diana refused to move and locked gazes with the muscular demon as he tried to make sense of the memories whispering inside his head.

'You know, don't you?'

'I see something in you, but I can't put my finger on it.' The Ripper confessed as he cast a glance up at Qamar who was gasping or breath with two of the remaining robed figures tending to his wounds.

'Maybe this will help?' Diana offered as she ripped open her shirt, exposing a gruesome series of scars across her torso.

'Impossible.' The Ripper gasped as his eyes traced the maze of jagged scars that covered every inch of Diana's skin.

'Say it.' Diana hissed as she re-buttoned her shirt. 'Tell me who I am.'

'You died.'

'Yes, my body died, but you denied me my meeting with Death.'

'You're one of the whores that kept me alive.' The Ripper smirked, his dismissive tone clearly annoying Diana. 'Which one were you?'

'Would you know me, even if I spoke my name?'

'Probably not. You weren't important enough to remember.'

Diana's eyes darted to the discarded sword and saw Kimberley hugging the shadows, making her way to the weapon. Knowing she needed to keep The Ripper's attention on her, she looked back to the demon and drank in his repulsive appearance.

'Your face has haunted me every single minute since you stole my life.' Diana barked, moving enough to keep his attention on her. 'I had a life ahead of me, one I could never experience thanks to you.'

'You were nothing. The Society gave you to me, the gift of tainted lives to keep me thriving in this world.'

'I was someone's daughter, someone's mother.'

'A dirty child born of selling your body to the lowest bidder? Your child was doomed the moment you opened your legs for a penny.'

The Ripper's ridicule fuelled the fires of a lifetime of unrecognised hatred. It had been that desire for finality that had driven Diana for so long. Having turned her back on the life *he* had denied her, she had found her camouflage and set about finding her way to right the wrongs of her murder. Diana was simply the name she had adopted and, if truth be told, the only remnant of her past life was the burning revenge that had kept her from fading into the ether of forgotten souls. Fighting back the desire to strike, Diana humoured The Ripper enough to keep his attention on her.

'You had no right, neither did they, in offering me like cattle for slaughter.'

'And now you serve alongside them?' The Ripper chortled, his jagged teeth shimmering in the firelight, still stained with the blood of the dead woman.

'A means to an end.'

'I must applaud your devotion. It could not have been easy to play this part for so long. Obedient slave to the very people who offered you to me.'

'It was necessary to bring you to this moment.'

'To what end? Surely, you can't think you can better me? You are nothing but a battered, lost, and broken soul. In fact, let's see who you really are.'

With a nonchalant wave of his hand, Diana was transformed back into the woman she had been over a hundred years before. Once again dressed in her Victorian garb, the strength of her posture immediately disappeared and she was once again a bruised and battered woman of the night. Bedraggled and weathered, her eyes lost their spark and she was as The Ripper remembered her.

'That's better.' He smirked. 'Less the powerful creature you have become and more the battered little whore I remember you as.'

'Make me look how you want. It doesn't change the fact I brought you here.'

'The Society brought me here.'

'With my guidance. It was me who reignited their passion and interest in the prophecy.' Diana pulled her attention away from her bloodstained dress, fighting every urge to lunge at The Ripper. 'If it wasn't for me, you would still be in a stone box waiting to come back.'

'Then you are more a fool than I thought.'

'I bided my time, studied your adversary and learned everything I needed without him realising. It led me to that blade, and only when I had that, did I convince that bastard up there to do my bidding.'

'Bitch.' Qamar coughed as he smeared blood on his chin trying to hold back his cough.

'Such determination, such drive and devotion. I must commend you for that, but like I say, it was wasted.' The Ripper moved closer to Diana like a stalking tiger. 'You don't have the power to destroy me.'

'And the same can be said of you.'

Diana stood firm as The Ripper towered over her. Despite her appearance, she held herself proud and waited for the attack she knew would come. When The Ripper took hold of her throat and lifted her into the air, she didn't even flinch. Instead, she held his gaze and stared with defiance into his lifeless eyes.

'Do I kill you again?'

'You can't.' It was Diana's turn to offer a smirk as she spoke. 'I am cursed to wander this earth, nothing more than a ghost of the past. There's nothing you can do to me other than play this game over and over again until you're banished from the earth and I can at last be free.'

'And you said you had learned everything about me.' The Ripper mocked, his tone catching Diana by surprise. 'You seem to have missed the fact I can do what I want with the souls I take. You're only still here because you were of no concern to me.'

'I'm already dead.'

'That you are, but I can still send you to a place worse than the existence you have endured.'

Had there been any blood pumping in her empty body, the colour would have drained from Diana's face. Eyes wide with a sudden surge of fear, she watched as Kimberley retrieved the sword and prepared to attack.

'Then why didn't you do that in the first place?'

'Because,' he moved her closer until their faces were almost touching. 'It is far more fun knowing you're tortured being surrounded by the lives you can never have and knowing you can never escape it.'

'That's a fate worse than hell.'

'Is it? There's only one way to find out.' There was nothing but pure evil in his eyes as The Ripper snarled at her. 'But before that, I must know one thing.'

'What's that?'

'How did it feel, learning you were no different to me?'

'I'm nothing like you.'

The Ripper dropped Diana as she answered and swiftly intercepted the sneak attack Kimberley had made. Ripping the sword from her grasp, he sent Kimberley flying to crash onto the raised platform across from Qamar. Crashing to the stone floor, he smiled as Kimberley slumped in an unconscious heap.

'You manipulated her life, taking any choice away from her.' The Ripper hissed as he toyed with the sword. 'You treated her as I treated you. Nothing more than a means to an end. Although, I expect it hurt all the more when you saw her as the daughter you never had.'

'I had a daughter.' Diana spat as she backed away.

'Ah yes, so you did. She didn't taste like you, though.' Tossing the sword to Diana, he allowed his words to have their effect before he attacked. 'I killed her the same night I fed from you. In fact, it was your love for her that led me to her, especially when that bastard constable disturbed my meal. Only seemed right to finish the night with what I had started.'

'You're lying.' Diana snapped as she caught the sword.

'You never searched for her? That does surprise me.'

'I didn't want to see what you had denied me.'

'I can show you her, if you'd like. Just like you, there's a bit of her still inside me.'

Diana was fuelled by the hate that had burned in her since the night of her murder. No longer thinking tactically, she surged towards her opponent with the tarnished blade gripped in both hands. Holding it high above her head, this was no longer about gaining her own closure. It was about avenging absolutely everything the demonic Ripper had taken from her.

She was a woman denied her life; a mother denied a daughter and more than everything; she was a soul denied closure.

The two of them met in the room's centre and exchanged a foray of parries and attacks that were almost impossible to follow. Diana had prepared and trained for this moment and used every ounce of strength and skill to weave her way around, over and alongside The Ripper. Moving with prowess and skill, her blade never found its mark and even when she thought she had the upper hand, somehow The Ripper would move away at the last second.

It was obvious he was toying with her.

Ignoring the screams of frustration in her head, Diana was relentless in her attacks and pressed forward. Slashing, driving and stabbing the sword ahead of her, she screamed in anger as The Ripper once again dismissed her attack with a simple flick of the Moon Blade in his hand. Deflecting the sword, he stepped to the side again as Diana thrust forward.

'Have you had enough?' The Ripper taunted as she lost her balanced and crashed to the floor at his feet.

Moving with astonishing speed, Diana felt nothing as the Moon Blade ripped through her right arm, severing it at the elbow. Seeing her hand, still gripping the sword, drop to the ground she knew she was done for. Despite everything, she had failed, and yet it still felt like a victory. She had faced the demon that had condemned her to this torment.

'I won't give you the satisfaction of begging.'

'Good.' The Ripper hissed as he peeled her fingers from the handle of the sword and raised it into the air. 'Maybe I'll see you down there, but I expect you'll just be another anonymous face in the sea of souls in your own hell.'

With that, The Ripper drove the sword down, directing the blade towards her neck. Refusing to close her eyes and accept defeat, Diana locked gazes with her killer and waited for whatever new fate awaited her.

24

RESURRECTION

John, once again in the garb of the Raven, waited for a more familiar world to take shape around him. Instead, he found himself transported to a plateau in front of a curious building that looked to have grown from the floor. It stood a curious mix of crystal and pale stone. It was like nothing he had seen before. Peering beyond the building, John once again saw the shimmering dome in the centre of the impressive city.

Even at a distance, John could see the strange array of architecture that reflected every era of human history. Greek, Roman, Mesopotamian and many grand styles perfectly complimenting one another.

'What is this place?' John asked, sensing Azrael behind him. 'That's twice you've brought me here.'

'It is my home.'

'Heaven?'

'Hardly!' Azrael scoffed as he moved to join John. 'This is where I bring those souls whose fate is as yet undecided. This building here is my home, the Cacna.'

'So, why are we here?'

'Because of you.' Azrael held out his hand.

'What?'

'Your coat.'

Unsure of where this was heading, John pulled down his hood, shrugged off the leather coat before handing it to Azrael. Without a word, Azrael took a step back and dropped the coat to the ground. After a few seconds, the coat burst into flames, forcing John to take a step back.

'What are you doing?'

'That Raven is dead.' Azrael replied flatly as the flames died down, leaving a pile of pale ash where his coat had been.

'I kept that coat for a reason.' John replied. 'It was a reminder of my past.'

'I know.' Azrael dropped to his knees and dragged his finger through the simmering embers, drawing odd shapes in the ash. 'And that is why this process is so important. What about the mask?'

'What about it?'

'Would you like a new face for the world to see?'

'I've grown fond of this one.' John mused as he unclipped the plague doctor mask and admired it.

'So have those who have seen it.' Azrael's words were laced with accusation. 'It was for the shadows, not for the world to see. But I can see why you like it, so you can keep it.'

Shifting his attention from his mask and back to Azrael, there was no hiding his surprise at what he saw. Pressing both hands into the pile of ash, Azrael pulled out a new coat, something far different from the brown leather John had become accustomed to. Once the coat was free, the clothes about John's body changed to match the new outfit. Form-fitting and tighter in fit, they were a strange mix of ink-black and silver trim, even more reminiscent of a Raven and yet far more modern in design than the Victorianesque outfit he was familiar with.

'A new Raven, for a new world?' Azrael offered John the coat. 'We return no longer tied to our past, but driven towards our future. Do you accept?'

Although there was no doubt he would accept, John revelled in the sheer look of panic on Azrael's face at his delay in snatching the coat from his hand. Taking pleasure from the sudden change, John turned his back on Azrael and once again admired the vast city that stretched out in front of him.

'You know I'll take it,' John finally offered. 'I just want to take a moment to savour this, whatever it is, as I expect I'll never get the chance to see it again.'

'You won't.'

'I feel my removal from the Knight's Bridge is only temporary. Whatever happens to me, when the end comes, it'll be back there, won't it?'

'Yes.' Azrael sighed behind him. 'There is nothing I can do to change that fate.'

'You should have told me.'

'Perhaps. But would it have changed anything? Would you have said no?'

'That's besides the point.' John groaned as he looked to the Pantheon building attached to the side of the impressive dome. 'You should have told me everything.'

'Maybe you're right, maybe you're not.' Azrael joined him and held out the coat once again. 'What's done is done. We look to the future now. What do you say we get back and right the wrongs of what passes with The Ripper?'

'Do I have a chance?' The coat surprised John with its lightness as he took it. 'If he now sits as the guardian of the gates, what are we going to find when we get back?'

'Hell on earth, I would expect.' Azrael sighed as he replaced his hood and prepared to take them back. 'But there's only one way to find out.'

Slipping the lightweight coat over his shoulders, John took a moment to admire his new look in the crystal walls of the Cacna building. Although the changes were subtle, he somehow felt more in tune with the Raven he was supposed to be. No longer a mishmash of past and present, he realised he was now an icon to the protector he was. Proud of his new appearance, John replaced the mask over his face and turned to face Azrael.

'Hell it is.' John remarked from behind the mask.

'You'll need this.'

Azrael held out a scabbard and sword for John to take. Admiring the weapon, John saw the pommel was a polished brass raven, while the handle itself looked to be made of the same polished marble as the surrounding buildings. Although simple, a knight of some sort centred the crossbar and, as he removed the blade from the scabbard, he realised it was the same tarnished metal as the other weapons he had seen.

'What's this?'

'That is the Altum Sword, a weapon gifted to me by the very people who sit in that dome. It is something I have cherished and yet never used.' Azrael swelled with pride as John tested the weight of the word in his hand. 'I would see you use it to right the wrongs we are both responsible for.'

'Can it kill him?'

'It is of the same dark magic as the tarnished blades, so yes, it can end The Ripper's reign.'

Catching the sunlight on the blade, John could see there were markings and letters beneath the pitting, but not enough was visible to make out the details. Dragging the narrow blade through the air in a figure-eight pattern between them, he suddenly felt they had a chance of winning this sordid game of death and destruction.

'I suppose it beats using two wooden sticks.' John chuckled as he replaced the sword into its scabbard. 'You have to admit, they were kind of appropriate for me.'

'You can still use them.' Azrael chuckled. 'But I suggest we use the sword more than your sticks.'

'Let's do this.'

Hanging the sword from his belt, John smoothed out the coat and cast one last glance back at the impressive city. Closing his eyes, John preferred to lock the memory in his mind rather than watch it fade away as Azrael transported them back to London. Feeling the familiar sensations of movement, the serene peacefulness of his surroundings changed, and he heard the rise and screams of panic and terror rising to greet them. Feeling solid ground beneath his feet, John opened his eyes and felt his heart sink at the sight before him.

Having not returned to the secret chamber of the Full Moon Society, Azrael had brought them back at the shrouded entrance to New Inn Street. With their backs against the rolling wall of mist, all John could see were the writhing and fighting bodies littering the floor as a scourge of demons bounced between their victims.

'What is this?' John gasped as he called the two escrima sticks into his hands.

'The gates are open.' Azrael sighed as he, too, called the familiar scythe to his own hands. 'They are feeding, becoming an army capable of surviving in the land of the living.'

Not wasting a moment to reply, John was about to launch an attack at the nearest demon when Azrael took hold of his arm.

'What are you doing?'

'We protect ourselves, nothing more.' Azrael barked as he pushed past John and set about navigating a path between the feeding demons.

'What about these people?'

'They're still alive, for now.' Azrael explained as John fell into step behind him. 'The longer they are exposed to the Demonites, the less chance we will have of saving them.'

'Then we should stop them.' John argued as he ripped one creature from its perch atop a young woman and threw it across the street.

'For each one we slay, another is born. The gates are open, to close them, we must reclaim the throne.'

'The Ripper?'

'Exactly.' Azrael drove his scythe through the air as a Demonite attacked.

Cleaving the creature in two, both halves were lost among the sea of bodies and creatures. Offering John nothing more than a curt nod, Azrael made his way towards the entrance into the old schoolyard. Having been unconscious when they had arrived, John followed blindly, hoping that Azrael was leading him back to the chamber and the unfinished business he had with The Ripper.

'Azrael!' A shrill voice shrieked over the chatters and screams.

Stopping dead in his tracks, John saw Azrael's hands tighten around the wooden handle of his scythe.

'Go through the gates and turn right. There's an old staircase, it'll be open, that'll take you down to him.'

'What are you going to do?' John pressed as Azrael turned to face the direction of the shrill voice.

'I'm going to redress the balance, and keep her busy.'

It was the first time John had seen Amber and her appearance stole his attention. Dressed in a sleek, form-fitting catsuit, her head of black hair was tied in a ponytail behind her head and her smooth brown skin showed no signs of having been born of whatever hell these Demonites had come from. She could have been any woman, clearly a warrior in the wrong era, but she could have blended in among the living without a problem.

'Your pet was banished, bringing him back invalidates his claim to the throne.'

'As does your manipulation in placing your pet upon it.'

'Touche!' Amber sniped as she removed a spear from her back and extended it out in front of her. 'Must we really?'

'We must.' Azrael hissed from beneath his shadowed hood. 'Their battle is theirs, ours is ours.'

John watched in silent admiration as Azrael propelled himself up into the air, his long black cloak billowing behind him. Seeing the attack in slow motion, it surprised John how far Azrael had flown as he landed a handful of steps away from the Dark Angel Amber. Too far to hear what was being said, John longed to hear more, but sensed a movement in the corner of his vision. Acting on instinct, John intercepted another sneak attack and abruptly slammed both escrima sticks into the torso of an attacking Demonite.

Wasting no more time, knowing that Azrael had afforded him a chance to make his move, John sprinted along the street and through the open gate into the old schoolyard. Seeing more of the Demonites clambering out of a narrow staircase, John moved with haste and despatched the stragglers as he bounded down the stone steps and back into the subterranean chambers of the Society.

Guided by his senses, feeling the pull from his connection with Kimberley, John found his way to the open doors of the chamber without issue and launched through as The Ripper drove the sword down towards Kimberley's head.

'Stop!' John's voice echoed around the vast chamber and had the desired effect.

As all eyes turned to him, Kimberley's included, it was the expression on The Ripper's face that brought him the greatest satisfaction.

'Impossible.'

'Not really,' John offered as he sauntered towards his bemused audience. 'Seems we can all play dirty when we all disregard the rules.'

Kicking Kimberley away, The Ripper tightened his grip on both the Moon Blade and sword in his hand. Knowing his silent invitation had been accepted, John paid no attention to Diana as she moved to drag Kimberley away from the battle that was about to happen.

'I'll happily kill you again, for a third time.' The Ripper sneered.

'Less talk, this isn't some cheap monologue.' John quipped and attacked.

25

— · —

WHERE IT BEGAN

John's attack found its mark, the escrima stick in his right hand slamming into the side of The Ripper's head. Catching him off-guard, John landed and quickly followed up with a second strike. Hearing the satisfying crunch of bone, John was about to strike again when The Ripper launched the pair of them up into the air.

Rather than colliding with the ceiling, John found himself transported back to the all too familiar surroundings of Victorian London.

'This should be more to your liking.' The Ripper snarled as he released John, sending him tumbling to the ground.

Crashing into the cobblestone, John righted himself and quickly took in his surroundings. Seeing the broken fountain across the opening, John knew he was back where this had all begun, the very place of his murder. Turning his attention skyward, John saw The Ripper lower himself down from the sky and disappear behind the buildings out of view. Knowing the rat-runs of Whitechapel, John knew where The Ripper would be and stalked across the square.

Feeling the eyes of London on him, John scanned the open doorways and alleyways as he passed them but saw no sign of any people. Emerging into the main street, John stopped in his tracks at the curious display in front of him. The street was lined with a sea of unfamiliar faces, all facing in towards the roadway where The Ripper now waited for him.

'Don't you dare face me in the real world?' John shouted as he walked towards his opponent.

'The setting doesn't matter,' The Ripper replied as he waved his hand and the crowds turned their back on John as he stalked past them. 'It seemed more fitting to end it here, where it all began.'

Unnerved by the crowds turning away, John steeled himself and kept his attention on The Ripper as he moved along the street. Casting the escrima sticks aside, John withdrew the Altum Sword from its sheath and marched towards The Ripper. Locking gazes with the imposing demon, John filtered out every distraction and allowed his mind to settle on his powers and the fight ahead.

As the heavy sky came alive with flashes of lightning, the booming rumbles of thunder shook the floor, and with it, John sprinted the remainder of the distance between them. Reaching The Ripper, their weapons clashed between them, neither man yielding an inch as they came face-to-face.

'You're brave.' The Ripper spat across the locked blades.

'No, just a little stupid.' John grinned and slammed his elbow up into The Ripper's chin.

Unseen by the crowds now facing away, John and The Ripper used every inch of the open street. Moving with impressive speed and poise, John was renewed since his return from the Knight's Bridge. Feeling empowered by the sleek exterior of his new appearance, John dropped his weight low and launched up onto the face of an old public house. Defying gravity, John sprinted the length of the building and arced up and over The Ripper's head.

Surprised by John's nimbleness, The Ripper's confidence evaporated as he moved with haste to block his blade. Deflecting John's blade at the last second, the shimmering tip gouged a neat slash across The Ripper's bicep as John rotated away. Feeling the sting of pain, John saw the sudden surge of panic in his eyes and pressed harder with his attacks. Up, over, through and around, John moved like a man possessed as The Ripper did all he could to keep himself from feeling the sting of the Altum Sword again.

Fed by his newfound confidence, John pressed forward and found his attack thwarted. Falling into overconfident comfort, The Ripper sensed his next move and was quick to take the advantage. Allowing John's sword to cut closer than he would have liked, he saw John shift forward as he overcompensated with his balance. Taking hold of John's wrist, The Ripper crashed a solid fist into John's ribs and used the momentum to throw him across the street.

Unprepared by the sudden shift, John smashed through the window of the opposite building and now found himself in a dark and dreary workhouse. Surrounded by looms and machinery, John dusted himself off as The Ripper crashed through the same window and continued their fight.

The cluttered workhouse was not the place for their fight as they all but destroyed the memory of the old factory. Cogs and splinters of wood flew in every direction as the pair of them crashed through whatever got in their way. Feeling the sword slip from his grip, John wasted no time in picking up a piece of snapped steel machinery and using it to defend himself from a flurry of thrusts and attacks from The Ripper.

Armed with both the Moon Blade and the tarnished sword, John moved with desperation as he drove the shattered cog between them. Deflecting the longer blade of The Ripper's sword, he felt dismay as the Moon Blade hooked a path across his torso leaving a wave of fiery pain in its wake. Recoiling away, John fought dirty and hurled the broken cog before launching himself over a listing piece of machinery to reclaim his sword from the splinters of rubble.

Taking hold of the polished handle, John leapt over the listing machine and balanced himself among the support beams of the factory roof. Taking to the shadows, he watched in silence as The Ripper scoured the debris of the destroyed factory for any sign of him. Taking a moment to settle himself, John realised his coat was ripped and torn from the fight. Ignoring the telling fact The Ripper had come close, more than once, to landing a crippling blow, John prepared himself for another attack.

Moving just enough to catch The Ripper's attention, John waited until his opponent made his move. Knowing he would bound himself up towards the shadows, John waited until the demonic creature had launched from the ground, before he dropped down and intercepted his trajectory. Not expecting such a move, The Ripper had no choice but to absorb John's full weight as they crashed back down to the ground with John hammering the pointed raven pommel of his sword down on The Ripper's head.

As they crashed to the ground and split apart, John was on his feet in an instant preparing for the return attack that was sure to follow. Keeping himself low, John watched as The Ripper emerged from a pile of dust and debris from the shattered machinery. With his face marked with blood, John looked down at the bloodstained brass raven and smiled with satisfaction. Knowing any advantage would be short-lived, John surged forward and resumed his attacks.

Feigning an attack with his sword, John ripped it back at the last minute and sent The Ripper flying across the room with a solid kick into his chest. Colliding with the wooden doors, John followed The Ripper as he smashed through the doors and sent the gathered crowds into the street scattering like skittles.

Chasing his opponent through the doors, the crowds of unmoving people refused to move. Those that had been knocked aside simply lay where they had fallen, but no eyes watched as the fight resumed in the London streets. Bouncing along the street, John and The Ripper were entwined in battle, weapons bouncing off one another until, at last, John's blade gouged a jagged gash down The Ripper's face.

Recoiling back, fighting back the sting of pain, John smiled beneath his mask as he saw the seeping wound where the demon's eye had been.

'Enough of this charade.' The Ripper snarled as he wiped the blood from his face. 'You want power, I'll show you power.'

Backing away, The Ripper looked to the stormy sky as a pair of enormous wings erupted from his back. Stretching out either side of him, he offered a twisted smirk before launching up into the air. Craning his neck to keep The Ripper in sight, the demonic figure was lost as the sky was lit by a bright flash of lightning. Hearing the *whoosh* of air behind him, John turned in time to feel the solid fist that crashed into the side of his head, sending him rolling across the cobbled floor.

Dazed and fighting to keep the soaring Ripper in focus, John rolled himself over as an enormous piece of masonry smashed on the floor where he has been seconds before. Peppered by the pieces of stone, John scanned the skyline for any sign of The Ripper but saw nothing.

'What Raven cannot fly?' The Ripper mocked from a rooftop above. 'You were never the sentinel this world needed. You were nothing more than another lost soul.'

Another attack, silent until the last moment, and once again John was sent crashing into the gathered crowds of motionless figures. Pushing away from them, John caught movement in his peripheral vision and directed his attention in that direction as The Ripper swooped down to attack again. Moving out of desperation, John ducked low and then launched himself up into the air as The Ripper moved towards the place he had just been standing.

Driving the Altum Sword down, John felt the blade bite into the flesh of The Ripper's wing but it was not enough to thwart his movements. Doing nothing more than tearing the thin wing, John dropped to the ground and prepared himself for the next attack. Not wasting the time to search the stormy skies, John sprinted into the wide open square beside the shattered fountain and waited.

When it came, he was ready. Rather than waiting for the sounds of The Ripper's wings, he scoured the surrounding street for the demon's essence. Only when the frenzy of fear had subdued could his mind pick out the almost indistinguishable tendrils left behind as his hunter stalked around him. Knowing where The Ripper would attack this time, John feigned ignorance until the last moment.

Ducking to the side as The Ripper barreled through the air, John scooped the Altum Blade up and under his body, driving the shimmering tip into The Ripper's shoulder. Yanked off balance, John dug his heels into the ground and dropped his weight onto the opposite side, ripping The Ripper from his flight and sending him smashing down onto the cobblestone road.

Tearing himself away from the sword, John could only offer a masked smile of satisfaction as The Ripper's shirt hung open with a fresh wound across his right pectoral. Oozing blood, the Ripper paid the injury no mind as he turned and ran.

'Coward.' John hissed as he launched after his feeling adversary. 'How the tables turn.'

Too late, John realised The Ripper had been playing him. Keeping close on his heels, John had no time to react as The Ripper turned around and scooped the Moon Blade up diagonally. Returning the favour, John felt the sting of pain as the enchanted blade cut through the fabric and flesh along his right side. Recoiling away, John caught The Ripper's wrist as the Moon Blade thrust out towards his face. Locked together, the hooked nose of John's mask touched The Ripper's face as neither man was willing to break free.

'A valiant effort.' The Ripper snarled. 'But, you will always be the cast-off pup, never ready to face me.'

Feeling The Ripper's grip tighten. John made his move with astonishing speed. Dragging his gloved hand across the curved blade, the leather slipped free from his palm as he thrust his hand out and pressed his bare flesh onto The Ripper's forehead.

The moment their skin touched, both of them were torn from the memory of London.

26

ULTIMO PROELIO

D ragging them back through their shared memories, John brought them back into the ceremonial crypt of the Society. Unwilling to keep their battle on a metaphysical level, even deeper within the shadows of the afterlife, John summoned them back and watched with great satisfaction as the crypt took shape around them.

'Why are we back here?' The Ripper coughed as he wiped the blood from the jagged wound on his face.

'It's a fitting place for your end.'

'Or yours.'

Not waiting for a retort, The Ripper attacked and once again their fight resumed in the confines of the crypt. Despite the time that had passed in their memories of London, it was as if they had been gone only a matter of seconds. Kimberley was still recovering from being launched onto the raised platform, while Qamar was still being tended to by two of the robed worshippers. The only other person left was Diana, who sat slouched against the far wall in a state of shock as the tattered flesh from her severed arm had already begun decaying.

Catching the attacks, John had no time to take in any more of his surroundings as The Ripper's attacks increased in ferocity. Blocking, thrusting and parrying, John kept his attention fixed on the battered Ripper. Despite the myriad of injuries that now covered his body and face, he moved as if unaffected by any of them. With each thrust or movement, the torn flesh on his face danced like some macabre face mask.

Their furious fight stretched width and breadth of the vast chamber until John crashed into the throne in the centre of the room. As he stepped backwards, John felt the solid stone against his back. Without hesitation, The Ripper was on him in a second and pinned him into position with his full weight. Swiping the Moon Blade down the plague doctor mask, The Ripper neatly cut the mask in two and watched with satisfaction as the mask disintegrated falling to the floor.

'I can see the fear in your eyes.' The Ripper snarled, blood and spit dripping onto John's exposed face.

'And I can see the fear in the one you've got left.'

Reacting out of frustration, The Ripper slammed his forehead into John's face and sent stars dancing in his vision. Their fight was no longer about primal skill, this was now a fight of rage and hatred. Discarding his sword, John fought to hold back The Ripper as the muscular demon slammed his fist into John's face and neck relentlessly. Blow after blow, this was not the fight of a demon, but of a crazed creature intent on destroying the Raven.

'Leave him alone.' Kimberley's voice echoed through the chamber to no effect.

Overpowered by the powerful demon, all John could do was hold back The Ripper as much as he could. Still, his heavy fist slammed into John's head and the world closed in around him.

'You are nothing to me.' The Ripper hissed as he slammed his forehead into John's bloodstained face once again. 'The magic of these weapons may scar me, may bring to life that which has been dead for centuries, but that is all.'

Unable to reply, John's head swam with confusion as he felt his body growing weak. With what little strength he had left, he pushed back but once again felt The Ripper's weight trap him against the stone.

'You are nothing.' The Ripper screamed and slammed his elbow down onto John's collarbone.

Forced down by the power of the attack, John's legs buckled beneath him and he felt the strength leave his body. Dazed, overpowered and fighting to stay conscious, all he could do was look up at The Ripper as his wings once again folded into his back and he dropped to his haunches in front of him.

'What now?' John wheezed, his body slowly failing him. 'There is no end to this now.'

'Oh, but there is.' A twisted grin appeared on his bloodied face. 'A new sacrifice and a new prophecy.'

'Look how that worked out last time.' Despite his defiance, John's voice was weak and his words unconvincing.

Doing his best to resist, The Ripper pushed aside John's hands as he used the tip of the Moon Blade to cut open John's top. Pulling aside the fabric, exposing his chest, The Ripper leaned closer to whisper in John's ear.

'We are both of us, dead.' The Ripper hushed as he teased the blade across John's flesh. 'Life does not beat through our hearts, but they are a jewel of life. It's funny that we used another jewel to resurrect me and honour the prophecy, when we could have just kept it all with you.'

Feeling the searing heat on his chest, John arched his back and turned his head to the inverted dome ceiling to escape the waves of pain. Reaching for the discarded Altum Sword, The Ripper stamped his foot down on John's wrist, pinning his arm in place on the ground.

'There's no fight left in you. Accept it, you were never the one to stop me.'

With nothing left to offer, John knew he was done for. Already he could hear the tumbling water in the Knight's Bridge calling to him.

'Just promise me one thing.' John offered as The Ripper placed both hands on the Moon Blade to deliver the final blow.

'I owe you no honour in your death.'

'Still,' John forced a smile as he locked gazes with The Ripper. 'Promise me you won't hesitate.'

'What?'

John offered no reply. Instead, he let Kimberley give The Ripper his response as she drove the Altum Sword down into the back of The Ripper's neck. Hearing the sickening sounds of metal scraping along bone, The Ripper released his grip on the Moon Blade and surged backwards away from John. As the frenzied demon flailed to rip the sword free from his back, Kimberley dropped to her knees in front of John.

'What can I do?'

'I need to finish this.' John groaned as he scooped up the Moon Blade. 'Help me up.'

'You're in no state to fight.'

'This is the fate for only me, or him.' John replied as Kimberley helped him to his feet. 'One must fall.'

Pushing her away, John gripped the Moon Blade in his shaking hand as he staggered towards the flailing Ripper. Distracted by the ferocious pain of the sword in his back, The Ripper saw John too late. Rather than risk a renewed fight of desperation, John fought dirty and dragged the hooked blade across The Ripper's calves.

Severing the muscles in both legs, The Ripper dropped to his knees as John took his position behind him and pushed himself down onto the Altum Sword. Unable to do anything, John's weight forced the sword deeper into The Ripper's body until the blade burst of his stomach. Pressed down by John's bodyweight, The Ripper bent forward as the sword's tip sank into the stone floor. Pinned to the ground in an impossible position,

John struggled to keep on his feet as he staggered around to The Ripper's front.

'Your reign of terror is over.' John huffed as he took hold of The Ripper's collar.

Both men were broken. Beaten, bloodied and bruised, The Ripper remained pinned to the ground by the Altum Sword while John could barely hold the Moon Blade steady in his hand. Watching from across the room, Kimberley could see the level of John's sacrifice, all that he had lost to honour his oath to Azrael. Overcome with emotion, she watched as John offered no words and simply thrust the Moon Blade into The Ripper's chest with all the strength he could muster.

Unable to fight back, The Ripper raised his head to stare into John's eyes as the hooked blade pressed through bone and flesh. Pressing his free hand into The Ripper's chest, he found the lifeless heart of crystal and pulled it free.

'You deserve an end as macabre as this.' John snarled as he yanked the crimson heart and The Ripper slumped lifeless in front of him.

'What have you done?' Qamar shrieked as John staggered away from The Ripper.

Unsteady on his feet, Kimberley rushed to his side and helped him across to a burning bowl of oil on the far side of the chamber. As they reached the crackling fire, Qamar foolishly pushed his aids aside and dragged himself down the staircase down from the raised platform. Resting against the wall, John admired the intricate beauty of The Ripper's heart in his hand as he held it over the burning flames.

'A burnt jewel, a hell demons throne, both twins will meet a fight.'

Without ceremony, John dropped the heart into the bowl of flaming oil and watched as the fire consumed the crimson heart. Bathing the chamber in a blood-red glow, the pair watched as the heart sank into the oil until there was nothing left breaking the bubbling surface of the liquid.

'Is it done?' Kimberley quizzed as John turned to look at Qamar who was all but rolling himself down the stairs.

'There's one way to know.' John replied as his attention fell to the stone throne. 'Time to take my place and put things right.'

'It's not your prophecy.' Qamar hissed as he dragged himself across the floor towards them. 'You have no right to take his place.'

'I have no care for whatever power this brings.' John barked as he walked to the throne. 'I will happily forsake these powers once I have righted his wrongs.'

'That's not your choice to make.'

'It is.' John boomed as he reached the seat and took one last look around the room.

Seeing Diana on the ground, the decay that had begun at her severed arm now covered most of her body. Seeing her as the woman in the alleyway, John had a million questions for her, but now was not the time. Offering no theatrics, no flamboyant display as The Ripper had, John simply sat on the seat and closed his eyes.

The moment his body connected with the stone, the world around him froze in place. As his body absorbed the dark magic of the throne, he felt all signs of his battle with The Ripper disappear. Charged and reinvigorated, John took a moment before opening his eyes again and taking a moment to take in his surroundings. Seeing Qamar mid-crawl, his attention fell to The Ripper's corpse pinned to the ground by the enchanted sword. Stalking from the throne, his body no longer battered and broken, John towered over The Ripper in a handful of long strides.

'It's time to end this once and for all.'

With nobody else to hear his words, John ripped the sword from the Ripper's body and delivered a purposeful strike that severed the demon's head from its body. Unmoving, still frozen in position, John took hold of The Ripper's had and pulled it to him as he turned his back on the unmoving body and marched to the exit of the ceremonial chamber.

Leaving the carnage of his battle behind him, John made his way back up into the courtyard of the old school and out into the street filled with Demonites. Passing the frozen creatures, John found Azrael and the Dark Angel Amber in the midst of a furious fight surrounded by creatures. Gripping The Ripper's severed head in his hand, John took a second to compose himself and let the frozen world come to life again around him.

In an instant the street was alive with movement and pan-icked screams, yet everything fell silent when he projected his voice for all to hear.

'It is done.' Was all he said as all eyes turned to face him.

27

— · —

DESPERATE MEASURES

'E nough.' John yelled as he held The Ripper's head out in front of him. 'The gate is mine. Now, back to your prison demons.'

For a moment, John wasn't sure the Demonites had heard him, or maybe the prophecy was not yet fulfilled. Feeling all eyes on him, the Demonites slowly turned their attention back towards the school and moved with reluctance.

'Stay where you are.' Amber shrieked as she stalked towards John. 'This bastard has no sway. The prophecy is not his.'

'Amber.' Azrael protested as he followed, hot on her heels. 'This is not the way.'

'Enough with your pitiful rituals.'

Reaching him, Amber rotated her spear in the air and drove it at John's chest. Releasing his grip on The Ripper's head, he ripped the Altum Sword from his side and moved to block the attack. It was a futile and pointless move as Amber's attack never reached him. The tip of her weapon hung in the air inches from his heart, the look of frustration on her face told him it had not been her choice to hold her weapon just out of striking distance.

'What is this?' She snarled through gritted teeth.

'Despite your passion, this is not our fight.' Azrael offered as he moved to her side. 'Although you have manipulated everything, you have no control.'

'You defied the rules. What makes you different from me?'

John could see the strain on Amber's face, the sweat beading on her forehead as she fought to press her spear through whatever magic stopped her from finding her mark. Revelling in the sudden change of circumstances, John nudged The Ripper's head to Amber as he moved away and watched her stagger forward.

'I worked to redress the imbalance you had created.' Azrael smirked as removed his hood and allowed the skin to grow over his exposed skull.

'I'm pretty sure that must piss you off even more.' John goaded as Amber righted herself.

'Meaning what?'

'Your Ripper there was easily better than me. I had no chance of beating him.'

'And yet there he is.' Amber pierced the discarded skull and lifted it into the air on the tip of her spear. 'This would say different.'

'Only because I was given a second chance, thanks to you.'

'You gave me the means to bring him back from the Knight's Bridge. Without your betrayal, I could never have given him that.'

Amber struck again, this time kicking out and once again finding her attack thwarted from finding its mark.

'How can this be fair?' She seethed, backing away as the waves of Demonites marched their way back into the chamber.

'Seems two wrongs do make a right.' John chortled as he tested the limits of whatever protection he had from Ambers spear and moved closer to her.

'Enough of this.' Amber shrieked as she tried again to attack to no avail. 'Face me rather than hiding behind that veil of fear.'

John's response was to laugh, a response that left Amber stunned and furious. Still unable to strike, she was about to launch another flurry of attacks when Azrael's scythe stealthily hooked around her neck. Feeling the curved blade across her throat, Amber thought better of it but kept her attention locked on John as she spoke.

'This was not, and never will be, our fight.' Azrael warned as he moved to John's side. 'These are not battles for our kind, Reapers and Dark Angels.'

'Says who?'

'You know who.' Azrael's words were laced with warning and John saw Amber stiffen. 'Would you prefer we present ourselves for judgement?'

John read Amber's body language and saw that whatever judgement Azrael spoke of was something Amber was not too keen to embrace. Twisting over the scythe, John watched as Azrael waited patiently for a reply from Amber. Around them the crowds of Demonites had thinned as they marched into the grounds of the old school.

'What will happen to these people?' John eventually asked as he looked at the petrified woman curled up in the foetal position a little way to his side.

'I will make this nothing more than a bad dream for them.'

'So much for adhering to the rules, you're the one interfering now.' Amber accused as she glared at John.

'You've infected this place with your Ripper's pets. They should not be tainted by the shadows of your deceit.'

Azrael brandished the scythe in his hand before performing some impressive display of swordmanship with the weapon. Arcing the wooden handle and hooked blade in the air above his head, John gasped as the heavy crimson clouds collapsed down to the ground. Shielding himself instinctively from the collapsing ceiling of thunderous red clouds, he heard Azrael laugh as the clouds crashed to the ground and dissipated around him.

'They will have no memory of this.' Azrael warned as he tapped the tip of his scythe on the ground, turning the red clouds a shade of dark green.

'Maybe in their nightmares.' Amber goaded and Azrael was on her in an instant.

Pressing the blade against her chin, their faces almost touched, but she never took her eyes off John. Holding back his anger, Azrael hissed loud enough for both Amber and John to hear his warning.

'You should return to your master.'

'Or else what?' She turned her attention and pressed her neck down on the mottled blade. 'Would you dare to challenge me, and bring this stupid charade to an end?'

'You'd like that, wouldn't you?'

'More than you know.' Amber hissed as she gripped the shaft of her spear. 'So?'

'I won't give you the satisfaction.' Azrael stepped away and rested the scythe on the ground by his side. 'You'd better answer your master's call.'

Pointing back towards the school, John caught sight of movement against the flow of the final Demonites making their way back into the chamber. A sudden change in direction drew his attention and John immediately turned as he saw Kimberley pressing through the Demonites, flanked either side by the robed worshippers and more importantly, Qamar struggling to stay on his feet behind her.

'What are you doing?' John barked as moved to intercept them.

'Not a step closer.' Qamar warned as he pressed the bloodied dagger that had been in his stomach against Kimberley's throat. 'One more, and I'll slit her throat.'

'Do it.' Amber hissed and John reacted on instinct by slamming his elbow into her cheek.

'Shut up.' John hissed as he levelled his gaze at Qamar.

His skin was drained of colour and the robed figures were helping keep Kimberley restrained while he struggled to stay standing with the knife held in his shaking hand. Weighing up his options, John could not find a way to get to her and knew any attack would simply lead to Qamar dragging the blade across Kimberley's throat.

'This isn't how it should be.' Qamar's voice was shaky. 'He defeated you. You dishonour the prophecy by coming back.'

'You are mistaken.' Azrael warned as he dropped his scythe across Amber's chest to keep her from moving. 'The prophecy was honoured, despite her attempts to alter the course.'

'Give me his heart.' Qamar interrupted. 'I will fulfill the prophecy.'

'It's gone.'

'Lies!'

'Believe what you want.' John hissed as he levelled his sword at Qamar. 'Touch her and I'll kill you where you stand.'

'More innocent blood spilled by the so-called protector of the living.'

There was a look in Qamar's eye that told John everything. This was a desperate attempt of a man to hold onto something he had already lost, and he knew it. John knew Qamar would act, the slightest movement, the flicker of muscles in Qamar's wrist stood out like a beacon of his intention as the world move din slow motion.

'John, no.' Azrael's voice fell silent as the world moved in painfully slow motion.

All his senses were on fire as John surged forward while Qamar drove the knife into the air and pointed the tip down towards Kimberley's chest. John's movements were as laboured as Qamar's. With each step he took, the knife inched closer to Kimberley with her powerless to react. To his side, Azrael kept Amber at bay, while her face was a mix of devilish pride and admiration for Qamar's act of pure desperation.

Willing his body to respond faster, John fought with his muscles but felt no increase in speed as he slowly closed the gap between him and Qamar. Attention fixed on the descending blade, John moved to reach out for the gilded handle and intercept it from finding his mark and all the while Kimberley simply looked at him, a look of pure terror on her face.

Reaching the pair, John pushed to extend his arm but watched on powerless as the knife sank into Kimberley's chest. As the knife pressed through her flesh, the resistance against his movements eased and time returned to its normal speed. In an instant, Kimberley's yelp of surprise filled the air as she sagged forward into John's arms, Qamar's knife slipping out of the jagged wound.

'Kimberley!' John hushed as he lowered her to the ground. 'I'm so sorry.'

'Blood for blood.' Qamar proclaimed from behind him.

John acted on instinct, fuelled only by hate and anger. Without looking to find his point of aim, John pushed upwards and swiped the Altum Sword through the air as he moved. Despite the blade passing through flesh, muscle and bone, the force of his strike left John feeling no resistance at all. As the sweeping sword completed its arc, John glared at Qamar and revelled in the look of surprise on the man's face.

'Blood for blood indeed.' John hissed as Qamar's rigid body slumped to the ground and his head rolled from his neck to rest in front of Amber.

'John?' Kimberley's voice sounded weak.

Paying no more attention to Qamar, he dropped to Kimberley's side and scooped her head into his lap. Already her skin was pale and her top was stained with blood that oozed from her hole in her chest. Gasping for breath, she took John's hand, her blood smearing his pale skin as he she held him tight.

'I don't want to die.'

'Azrael?' Looking up to the visage of death and read the regretful expression on his face. 'Don't give me that, we brought her into this.'

'That isn't how it works.' Azrael protested, keeping his scythe pressed across Amber's chest.

'Do something.' John was awash with guilt and regret as he looked back to Kimberley's pale face. 'She deserves better than this.'

'Maybe she's better off away from you.' Amber taunted as she pushed aside Azrael's weapon. 'You cursed your bloodline the moment you became embroiled in matters far beyond you.'

'Watch yourself.' Azrael warned as she moved out of his reach.

'Let her speak.'

'Amber!' A sudden voice boomed and in an instant all confidence and self-assuredness evaporated from Amber. 'It is time for you to return.'

'But I'm not done.' Her voice sounded different, less confident and almost scared.

'Listen to your master's call.' Azrael mocked as he stalked past her to join John.

'My Dark Angel,' the voice continued, echoing off the faces of the surrounding buildings. 'It's time for you to return,'

Watching Amber torn, she took a moment to compose herself before turning her back on the trio and stalked back into the courtyard of the old school. Surrounded by the sea of unconscious partygoers, John held Kimberley's hand as tight as he could, both their hands smeared with her blood.

'Can't you do anything?' John struggled to find the words to say.

'I can offer her peace.' Azrael replied. 'I can make sure she gets where she belongs.'

'I don't want to die.' Kimberley stammered, tears falling down her face as her body grew cold and her vision started to fade. 'Please. I'm not supposed to die yet, am I?'

Azrael struggled to find an answer as he placed his hand over John and Kimberley's entwined fingers.

'No path is guaranteed. John's ended too soon, as does yours.' Azrael cleared his throat. 'I fear it is the curse of your bloodline.'

Sharing the somber moment, John gripped Kimberley's hand as he felt her grip loosen as the life slowly slipped away from her.

'I'm so sorry.' John croaked. 'I never meant to curse you with this, you deserve so much more.'

In the eerie silence of the street, nobody spoke as Azrael replaced the hood over his head and assumed his mantle as Death, guardian of souls.

28

A NEW SACRFICE

'There has to be something you can do.' John pleaded as Azrael watched from the deep shadows of his robes. 'This isn't how it should be.'

'As you have your duty, I too have mine.' There was a coldness to Azrael's voice as he spoke. 'Her fate will be decided by the council.'

'Decided? Her life has surely led to peace.'

'Her contact with the Ripper, her time in his memories, has left its mark.'

'That's bollocks!' John snapped and launched to his feet.

John was on Azrael in a heartbeat, had they shared one, and soon he stood glaring into the deep shadows of the hood. Knowing Azrael's skinless was face disguised in the darkness, John called the plague doctor mask back over his face and steeled himself. There was no way he was going to leave Kimberley's fate to a decision for those who didn't know her. Preparing himself, John was caught off-guard as Azrael simply thrust out both hands and shoved him hard in the chest.

Staggering backwards, John was no longer stood in the London street but found himself once again in the familiar surround of the interview room in the Nuthall. Facing the solid door, he heard Kimberley's voice and snatched his attention around.

'I won't say I believe what you're saying, but I believe you do.' Kimberley looked up from her notes. 'If you're alright talking about it, I'd like to ask some more questions and see if I can't get through what you believe is true and find what is actually the truth?'

'Whatever you like, Kimberley, I'm happy for you to waste some time trying to decipher something that isn't there.'

'Did you have any siblings?'

'No, I was an only child. My dad got injured in the factory after I was born, almost killed him, but it meant he couldn't have any more children.'

'And your mother?'

'She was lost.' John struggled to hide the sudden wave of pain that boiled from his stomach. 'She did everything she could to support my old man, but she had her demons. The year I joined the police, they found her in the Thames, drowned in a drunken stupor.'

John knew this moment. It had been the first time their paths had consciously crossed and put them on the course that had led to Kimberley lying dead at his feet. Muting out the conversation, John longed to be free from the Nuthall. Stalking to the door, he gripped the handle and ripped it open. To his surprise,

Diana was stood behind the door, no longer the well-dressed, immaculate woman she had been at the hospital, but now the festering and decaying representation he had glimpsed in the chamber.

'I was hoping you'd want free from there.' Diana offered as she waited John to compose himself.

'What are you doing here?'

'There are things we need to speak about, and this may be the last chance I have to explain why.'

John fought the urge to take Diana by the throat. The fact she looked broken and completely beaten helped in curbing his urge to hurt her. Choosing not to act on his instincts, he took a moment to compose himself before answering, all the while Kimberley and the memory of himself continued in muted conversation.

'Why should I even waste time listening to you.'

'Because I want you to understand why that was necessary.' Diana pointed to the pair in conversation behind John. 'And perhaps then you'll hate me a little less.'

'I'll listen,' John sighed. 'But I make no promise about how I'll react.'

'That's all I can ask.' Diana stepped back from the door. 'Shall we take one last walk through this place?'

'Lead the way.'

Stepping through the door, John allowed the plague doctor mask to disappear from his face and walked by Diana's side as the Nuthall hospital was now open to them. Every door they passed through was unlocked and apart from the memories left behind in the interview room, there was only the pair of them working their way through the labyrinth of corridors. As they walked, John remained quiet, and listened to what Diana offered.

'You and I have been connected since the night we died.' Diana explained as they walked. 'That night when The Ripper fed from my soul, you stopped him from claiming every part of me. That's the reason I stand here as I am.'

'What are you?'

'I am a lost soul.' Diana explained as they stepped into the vast open space of the main accommodation block. 'Where The Ripper would normally drain everything from his victims to sustain his fetid life, I was never cursed with that empty end. When you disturbed his feeding, I was left trapped between the worlds.'

'Like me.'

'In some ways yes, in others no.' Diana looked at the vast skylight high above. 'You were left with a purpose, with a drive and motivation that I lacked. You were never lost.'

'I felt lost.'

'That's how you made it for yourself.'

'I'm not the only one.'

'That's true.' Diana confessed as she resumed walking. 'Your grief and confusion was the opportunity I had searched for and when I found you, I knew you would be the means to the end I desired.'

'How long have I been part of your plan?' John snapped as they progressed through to Diana's old office. 'How long has Kimberley been part of that plan?'

'That's where my guilt lies. With Kimberley, not you.' Diana's response was surprisingly honest, leaving John shocked. 'You made your choice to exist in our world, she did not. When I found you searching for The Ripper, I watched from the shadows willing you to succeed when you faced one another.'

'I succeeded.'

'No, you merely postponed the finality I needed from the Ripper's demise. When you banished him to the Zassuru crypt, I knew you were not the one to kill him.'

'I have killed him.'

'But, would you have if I hadn't done what I did with Kimberley?'

'Perhaps.'

'Come now, John, we both know the answer to that. The moment you surrendered yourself to the Nuthall, you severed everything you had, and I knew it would take an immense catalyst to bring you back.'

'How long have you manipulated her?'

'Her whole life.' Diana sank into the chair behind her desk, the weight of her decisions clear in her posture and tone. 'Even as a child, I manipulated her life to bring her to you when the moment was right.'

'How dare you?'

'You made me.'

'Don't shift this onto me!' John slammed his hands onto the desk. 'You could have told me who you were, explained things to me.'

'Would you have listened?' Diana retorted. 'You were never open to anything of your past life. If I had shown myself, you would have gone even deeper inside yourself.'

'You don't know that.'

'I do. You do too!' Diana was right, she had spent so many years studying John that he knew she was right. 'It's why I would never risk you touching me, I always kept myself away in case you found the way to penetrate my memories and see the truth of who I was.'

John played every memory of his interactions with Diana in the hospital and realised how obvious it would have been had he been conscious enough of his surroundings to see. In the shortest flicker of memories, John realised how right Diana was and how much he had disconnected himself from the Raven when he had surrendered himself to confinement.

'It still isn't fair what you did to her.'

'You're not wrong.' Diana confessed as she locked gazes with John. 'It was, perhaps, the one thing that kept Qamar from fully trusting me.'

'How could you have spent so long in the company of people who wanted to defile the earth by unleashing The Ripper?'

'It was a means to an end. I needed to bring him back to face the final retribution and answer the prophecy if I was to have any hope of peace. I will not say it was easy, but it was necessary.'

Diana explained. 'You can't say you haven't done things that were distasteful, for the right reasons.'

'We aren't the same.'

'And we also aren't so different.' She countered calmly. 'I know I will never earn your trust.'

'Damn right.'

'But I hope I will earn your understanding. You always had an end in sight, some finality to the oath you made to Death. I had nothing.'

'It doesn't excuse sacrificing someone so innocent.'

'Was she innocent?'

'Don't go there!' John glared at her.

'You're right. Any guilt she carries was forced upon her by me, by you and by them.' Diana sighed.

'And because of that, she faces an unfair judgement.'

'Qamar always mocked me for my maternal affection towards Kimberley. He knew my past haunted me, but never knew the true extent, until it was too late.'

'But you didn't do a good enough job with him, did you?' John was quick to counter. 'You accuse me of leaving unfinished business with The Ripper in the Zassuru, and yet you did the same with Qamar. Because of it, he took her life.'

'I'm sorry.'

'That's not good enough!' John boomed, the memory shaking around them at the sound of his powerful voice. 'An apology from either of us changes nothing.'

Diana remained silent as she sat behind the desk and toyed with a pendant around her neck. Rolling the curious silver emblem between her fingers, she chose her next words with care.

'We are both guilty in this, and yet there is something we can offer.' Removing the chain from her neck, she placed it on the desk. 'What life is left in me can sustain just enough to keep her from the clutches of Death.'

'To what end?' John asked as he eyed the strange pendant.

In the light of the sparse office, he could make out the shape of something similar to a Norse rune. Reaching for the pendant, Diana grabbed his hand and locked gazes with him.

'This is what is left of my life.' Diana hushed. 'I am done with it now, I have avenged my death. Giving it to her, will offer her enough time for your to make your own amends.'

'How am I supposed to do that?'

'Give her what you so easily surrendered when you offered yourself to the Nuthall. You've honoured your oath to Death, let someone else assume the mantle of their protector.'

'Kimberley?'

'Better that than a tainted judgement where the dark tidings of The Ripper could still condemn her in the afterlife.'

'I'm not sure what's worse.' John confessed as he saw the light and life fading from Diana's eyes.

'It is yours to give. Your time as the Raven is over, and that is your one offering to right the wrongs we have both inflicted on her.'

Diana suddenly convulsed and dropped back into her seat. Clutching at her chest, John could only watch as Diana's body released its grasp on what little life had been left in her. Before his very eyes, he watched Diana progress through the delayed process of death until there was only a shrivelled and lifeless corpse left on the chair with her empty eyes looking up to the heavens.

Dropping his gaze to the pendant, John felt overcome with emotions he had not felt for years. In the weeks since meeting Kimberley, everything he had known had been flipped upside down. Knowing his time was limited, John snatched the pendant from the desk and, as was always the case, the memory faded around him.

Finding himself once again standing in the eerie street, John turned to look at Azrael.

'Don't take her yet.' John commanded as he thrust out the pendant at Azrael. 'There's something I need to do.'

29

---·---

MOURNING

'How did you come to have that?' Azrael hissed as he took Diana's pendant.

'It was an offering from Diana.'

'Diana?'

'To make amends for all of this.' John looked down at Kimberley's lifeless body on the ground.

'This will only delay her death, there's barely an hour left of life in this.'

'That'll be enough.'

'Enough for what?' Azrael offered the pendant back to John. 'There can be no deviation of her path to Altum.'

'There can, if you humour me.' John offered his familiar wry smile. 'My oath to you is served, right?'

'Yes.'

'But we both know the Full Moon Society is now scattered to the wind and will remain a threat. They're not simply going to roll over and forget all that has happened here.'

'But The Ripper has been destroyed.'

'Are you telling me that's the only threat from that Amber woman and the place she comes from?'

'You know the answer to that.' Azrael mused as he looked around at the street filled with troubled souls laid all around.

'And there must always be someone to act as your Hand.'

'Are you offering to keep your position?' Azrael knew what was coming, but pushed John all the same.

'Not unless she refuses your offer. I want to use what's left of Diana's life, to give Kimberley the choice you once gave me.'

'It can't be that way. Before I make her that offer, you must surrender your position.'

'That's fine. I'd rather give her than chance than hold onto mine.

'There can never be two. An offer can only be made when I am no longer supported and find myself alone in my role.' Azrael sighed as he watched John drop to his knee by Kimberley's side. 'If she assume the mantle of my Raven, then your fate will be eternity in the Knight's Bridge. Is that something you are content with?'

'My fate will be what it is, I made that choice a long time ago. Kimberley's fate has never been her own, she deserves better than that.'

'Fine.' Azrael huffed and took the pendant from John. 'If she assumes the mantle of the Raven, and becomes my hand, I will accept her.'

John moved away as Azrael fastened the silver necklace around Kimberley's neck. The moment it was fastened, John saw movement on Kimberley's face as she blinked away the strange sensation of death that had taken her and took a moment to make sense of what was happening. Overcome with guilt, John stepped away from the pair as Azrael talked in a hushed voice, keeping his words quiet enough for John not to hear.

Alone with his thoughts, no longer drifting back to the Nuthall, John felt a strange sense of pride and sadness as he looked around the desolate street. Although the crimson clouds had dissipated, the packed street remained deathly silent as bodies littered the street and pavements. What should have been a party atmosphere, and in fact had been not hours before, now felt like the scene of a massacre. Had it not been for the rise and fall of people's chest, John would have thought they were all dead.

Knowing that Azrael had done enough to erase the horrific events of the Demonite's rise, he couldn't help but wonder what had been going through the poor people's mind as the Demonites had tried to feed from their souls. Looking down at a young woman on the pavement, there was nothing to indicate the terror she would have felt as she now lay in a calm stupor on the ground.

Moving between the bodies, John made it to a small stall further up the street and stopped as he looked at the array of curiosities arranged on the stand. The stall was awash with curious items, but what caught his attention was an obsidian raven. Surrounded by all manner of trinkets, it was the shimmering jet-black bird that stole his attention. Reaching for the raven, John took it in his hand and admired the intricate detail of the bird's wings and face.

'John?' Kimberley's voice stopped him dead in his tracks as he composed himself to face her.

Clenching the obsidian raven in his hand, John turned around to see Kimberley making her way to him. Still wearing Diana's pendant, John struggled to meet her gaze as she reached him.

'Thank you.' Kimberley offered as she took his hand.

'You've nothing to thank me for.' John confessed, fighting to look anywhere but in her eyes. 'You should probably hate me for all the pain I've caused you.'

'Don't be daft, it's not your fault.'

'Of course it's my fault.' He argued, but was silenced as she placed her hand over his mouth.

'No silly remarks, no quips and certainly no guilt.' Kimberley interrupted. 'Azrael told me what you offered.'

John felt his heart sink. Whatever the outcome and Kimberley's choice, he knew this would be the last time he would see her.

'Don't tell me.' John answered as he pulled his hand away and took a step back. 'Regardless of your answer, I'm proud to know you are of my blood.'

'Shall we go?'

'Yes, please.' John choked.

'John, please.'

'I'm proud of you.' Was all he offered as Azrael moved to his side and the street disappeared.

Surrounded by darkness, John felt a solitary tear roll down his cheek.

'There's something I would show you, before your journey ends.' Azrael offered as they once again apparated in the marble city of Altum. 'I saw the wonder in your eyes as you took this in, and I would have you see it one time.'

John stood aghast as the enormous marble dome towered above him. To his side he saw the Pantheon building, but what stole his attention was the constant flow of water streaming down the smooth marble of the dome. Giving John a moment to drink in his surroundings, Azrael just watched with an unseen smile on his face. In Altum, regardless of his hood's shroud, Azrael never presented as the visage of Death. Rather than reveal his face, Azrael was grateful for the shadows of his hood, not wanting John to see the look of immense pride he had as he watched his companion struggled to comprehend his surroundings.

'Is this heaven?' John gasped as he looked behind him at the vast sprawling city of pale stone.

'Not quite.' Azrael mused. 'This is my place, the one where those unjudged souls come to have their fate decided.'

'In there?'

'Yes. That is the Hall Of Souls And Scales, not a place you'll ever see I'm afraid.'

'I don't think I'd want to.' John offered, the familiar twinkle appearing in his eye. 'You and I both know if I had to weigh up my life, the outcome would probably not be the prettiest.'

'You underestimate yourself, John Smith.'

'Do I?'

'I am Death, the Grim Reaper, the foreboding shadow, and yet I stand humbled in your presence.'

'Get lost.'

'I do. Never would I have thought your journey would have brought you here or followed the path you've trodden.' Azrael explained as he took a moment to admire Altum too. 'I always knew you were the right one to choose as my Raven.'

'You still regretted choosing me, more than once.'

'You're wrong.'

'Liar!' John mocked as he sensed the look of frustration on Azrael's face. 'Many times I frustrated you, just like on Tower Bridge.'

'You're like a child.' Azrael groaned. 'Ever the pain and yet the source of immense pride at what you've become.'

'Thank you.' The sincerity in John's reply caught Azrael by surprise. 'I mean that.'

'I'm sad I will no longer have a Raven by my side.' His declaration caught John off guard and all playfulness evaporated.

'She said no?'

'Yes.' Seeing John's disappointment, he was quick to keep John's attention from wandering. 'Come, there's something I've been wanting to do for a long time.'

Following Azrael in silence, they made their way through the amazing city of Altum, all the while John's mind raced with a thousand thoughts. After what felt like an age, having seen only a handful of faces in the streets, John realised they were back at the dark stone structure Azrael had brought him the last time. At odds with the serene pale beauty of the city, he turned his attention to the rough exterior of the building as Azrael opened the door and invited him to follow.

'What is it with this place?' John's voice echoed as they entered the vast building.

'The Cacna? I know it doesn't fit, much like me I suppose.'

The interior reminded John of a Japanese training room with pillars and two open levels looking down onto an open training room. Against the far wall, John saw three stone plinths illuminated by beams of sunlight pouring in through the ceiling. The ones at either end sat empty while Azrael's scythe hovered above the flat surface of the centre one.

'I've watched you grow as a warrior for years and always wondered one thing.'

'What's that?'

'Whether you'd be a worthy opponent.'

In a flash of lightning, the scythe was in Azrael's hand and at the same time John felt the weight of the Altum Sword in his hand. Without a word, Azrael attacked and the pair of them moved around the vast training area unleashing a flurry of blocks and attacks. Moving with the grace and speed their gifts allowed, this was like no fight John had ever experienced before.

For what he knew would be the last time, John called the plague doctor mask to his face and allowed himself to be the Raven for the final time.

While neither man had the intention to cause the other harm, there was no denying neither of them was willing to give any quarter to the other. Moving with impossible speed, John realised he had underestimated Azrael as the scythe whipped past his masked face too close for comfort. Despite his most valiant attempts, as their fight raged on, John could find no way to deliver any blow that could be considered victorious.

Consumed by the competition of their fight, John missed a single beat and it was all that Azrael needed. Moving the scythe with incredible speed, Azrael ripped John's feet from beneath him, sending him crashing to the floor. Before he could even react, John felt the cold metal of the curved blade pressed into his exposed neck.

'Do you yield?' Azrael quizzed as he removed the hood to show the victorious smile on his face.

'Ever the apprentice.' John replied, raising his hand in mock defeat as a Roman warrior would have in ancient times.

'But still a worthy opponent.' Azrael beamed as he took John's hand and hoisted him from the ground.

'What now?' John quizzed as he removed the leather mask from his face. 'I mean, how does it actually end?'

'I take you, if you're ready?'

'I'm ready.' John sighed, allowing the Altum Sword to fade from his hand. 'I've made my peace with everyone I needed to.'

Taking one last look at the plague doctor mask, John handed it to Azrael.

'In that case, it's time I presented you to Perseus.'

'Perseus?'

'Yes.'

As the Cacna building disappeared, John closed his eyes, not wanting to see the serenity of Altum fade around him. Feeling himself flying through the air, John waited for the sound of running water and rustling leaves.

30

ONE LAST PROMISE

J ohn didn't hear running water. Instead, the sounds that filled his senses were at odds with the peace of Knight's Bridge. Feeling solid ground beneath his feet, he wasn't sure if he dared to open his eyes as he tried to make sense of the surrounding sounds. They were familiar, a mix of engines, voices and general bustle. As his racing mind connected all the dots, he opened his eyes and was greeted by the familiar sight of London.

On the same rooftop he had observed Kimberley and Diana's meeting, John could see Trafalgar Square and the impressive architecture of the National Gallery on the far side of the square. For once, it wasn't raining and as he looked down, there was no sign that London had any knowledge of what had happened in the streets alongside the hidden chamber.

'How long has it been?' John quizzed as he tried to work out how long he had been absent.

'A few days.' An unfamiliar voice replied, startling John as he peered over the ledge

Turning on the spot, John scanned the rooftop but saw no sign of anyone. Raising his gaze, John stood dumbfounded for a moment as an unfamiliar figure stood perched on a narrow ledge above him. There was something familiar about the way they were dressed, a reminiscence of his own clothes as the Raven, but altogether different.

Where John had opted for a dark pallette of colour, whoever this was, wore a mix of light grey and black. Unlike John's plague doctor mask, the new arrival wore a slender mask, again echoing the style of John's Raven but without the slender beak.

'Who are you?'

'It's not been that long that you've forgotten me already, has it?'

There was something familiar about the voice. John could tell the mask was distorting their voice, but there was something about their tone and posture that teased familiarity.

'Let me make the introductions,' Azrael interrupted as the figure dropped to the rooftop in front of John. 'This is Perseus.'

'And who exactly is Perseus?' John quizzed as he admired the intricate mask covering their face.

'Maybe this will help.'

Reaching up, Kimberley removed her mask and beamed with delight at the look of surprise on John's face. Her skin no longer looked drained of life and her eyes sparkled in the daylight. It took every ounce of his self-control not to grab her and hug her. Rather than that, he turned his attention to Azrael and narrowed his eyes.

'You said she didn't accept.'

'I didn't,' Kimberley offered, while John continued to glare at Azrael. 'There's no way I could be who you were. That's not what I wanted to do. Your legacy is your own. Besides, I didn't want to live in your shadow.'

'Go on.' John answered through gritted teeth.

'Don't blame him. I asked him not to tell you.' Kimberley pleaded as she turned John to face her. 'I needed to tell you myself and ask you something.'

'Ask me what?'

'You told me it was a lonely job, being the Raven.'

'It is.'

'You made mistakes. We both know that. I don't want to make those mistakes. I want to be the sentinel you should have been. If you hadn't been left alone to find your own way.' Kimberley looked across at Azrael. 'It's been agreed that you can guide me. You can be my mentor and help me find my place as this.'

'Is that even possible?' John asked as he took in the intricate details of her impressive outfit. 'You did say there could only ever be one.'

'It would appear that cunning and cleverness runs in your bloodline.' Azrael replied as he moved to join them. 'There can only ever be one hand of Death, only ever be one Raven. By denying me, young Kimberley here circumvented the system.'

'Doesn't that bring unbalance?' While John was swelling with pride and relief, he couldn't shake the worries that raced through his mind. 'Aren't we no better than Amber and her devious ways of finding loopholes to exploit?'

'Do you know what I have learned in all of this?' Azrael looked at the pair of them. 'There is no balance in this game we play. We simply sit on a pendulum that swings one way and back. If I had continued to play by the rules, you wouldn't be here and The Ripper would have been victorious.'

'It doesn't make it right.'

'You'd rather the alternative?'

'Obviously not.'

'Then I say we wear that risk and instead of waiting to react, we are proactive in our approach.'

'She made you say that, didn't she?' John smirked as he read the expression on Kimberley's face. 'There's no way you'd have come up with anything that clever.'

'She's good, isn't she?' Azrael laughed as he held out the plague doctor mask for John.

'What do you say?' Kimberley pressed as she took a step back and left John to make his choice. 'Will you be by my side, be the mentor to me you never had?'

John was torn. Deep down inside, he had resigned himself to an eternity in the Knight's Bridge and in a way longed for the peace and serenity. On the flip side, Kimberley was right in the fact they had left him alone to find his own way. She was also right that he had made mistakes. While he knew she was wiser and smarter than him, he knew she could all too easily share the feeling of isolation and disorientating confusion that came with it.

'You remind me of someone.' John mused as he took the plague doctor mask from Azrael

'Yes, you!' Kimberley beamed, the broad smile appearing on her face.

'No, my wife. She was very much like you. She would be proud of you.'

'We met.' Kimberley declared. 'She was the one who brought me to you in the crypt, remember.'

'That alone tells me she would approve.' John declared, steeling himself and standing tall.

'You'll do it then?' Kimberley pressed, her youthful excitement bubbling over.

'Well, I'm hardly going to let you mess it up like I did.' John smirked as she slipped the plague doctor mask onto his face. 'Besides, it's a bit boring when you do this on your own.'

'It is done.' Azrael exclaimed. 'I'll leave you two to it.'

'Wait.' John boomed and turned his attention to Azrael. 'Before you go, I want to thank you.'

'For what?'

'For all of this. I know I wasn't exactly what you wanted, but now I have a chance to make Kimberley into the Hand you deserve.'

'You were exactly what I needed. She may be the future but without you, this wouldn't have come to pass.'

'Give me this one chance to be right, please.'

'No!' Azrael smirked. 'I'm glad you're wrong. Now, if you don't mind, I have been absent from my duties for too long.'

Without waiting for an answer, Azrael disappeared from the rooftop leaving Kimberley and John alone. Turning his attention back to the impressive view over Trafalgar Square, he moved to the ledge and rested his hands on the rough stone edge. Moving to his side, Kimberley replaced her own mask and lifted the hood over her head.

'I need to ask one thing.' John quizzed as he scanned the streets. 'What's with the name, Perseus?'

'This.' Kimberley replied as she pointed to the pendant and necklace that Diana had given her.

How he had missed it, John wasn't sure. Perhaps it was the fact the silver complimented the grey hues of her top, but there it was, as plain as day hung around her neck. Admiring the curious symbol, he waited for Kimberley to complete her explanation.

'I recognised it when I saw it. It's the Greek symbol for Perseus.'

'I know the story. Isn't it a bit, well, brave naming yourself after some ancient Demi-God?'

'It's just a name.' Kimberley replied. 'Besides, I needed something to make myself sound way cooler than you.'

'I'm just John Smith.'

'And I am no longer Kimberley Mansfield.' She declared as she stepped up onto the roof ledge. 'My name, is Perseus.'

Admiring the flamboyance and recognising the feigned confidence, John watched as Kimberley dropped from the rooftop. Raising his attention to the clouds, knowing somewhere Azrael was watching them, he shook his head and stifled a laugh.

'Was I really like that?' John groaned as he stepped onto the ledge himself.

Grateful for the fact Azrael did not answer, John smiled beneath his mask and performed his own display of acrobatics as he somersaulted from the roof and down to the street below.

Death's Hand as the Raven was no more.

In his stead, a new guardian had emerged.

An unknown sentinel.

Recruited by Death.

To protect humanity from evil.

Her name is...

PERSEUS

31

Bonus Artwork

What follows are some early concept sketches for scenes within the book. See if you can't picture these moments in the story you've just enjoyed.

The Raven ponders the future, still confined within the prison of both the Nuthall but also, his mind.

The face of The Ripper is born from the darkest parts of human fear. Born of darkness, he stands a true demon of Sub Terra with a desire to claim his rightful place in power above humanity. The essence of evil and truest demon of our version of Hell.

The Raven has an immense battle on his hands, one that sees the fate of humanity hanging in the balance. Ever the Hand Of Death, his heart has always been torn as to his strength and purpose...until now.

London's heart still beats, regardless of the era. This adventure dances the line between past and present and yet the very essence never really changes. No wonder the Raven finds his comfort in both sides of his own mind and memories.

What is Death if not a moment? The essence of everything hangs in the balance and yet finality is not ever what we dream or what it seems. Such a journey is unique to the soul presented before Death.

John Smith has a face, a name and a history. Beneath the mask he now finds himself in a very strange place and on a journey that has deviated from what he had ever expected. The world needs both John and the Raven.

The Battle Of Souls set about with the prophecy is an event of Dark Magic.

Printed in Great Britain
by Amazon